MW01612495

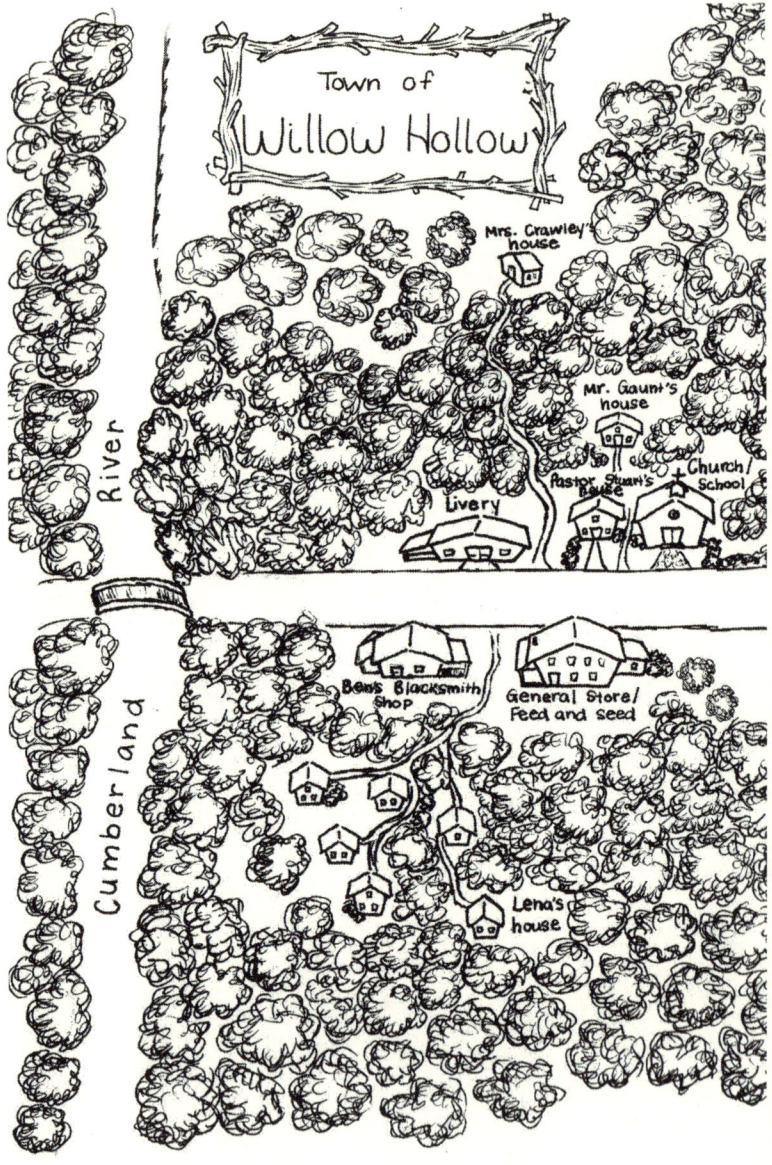

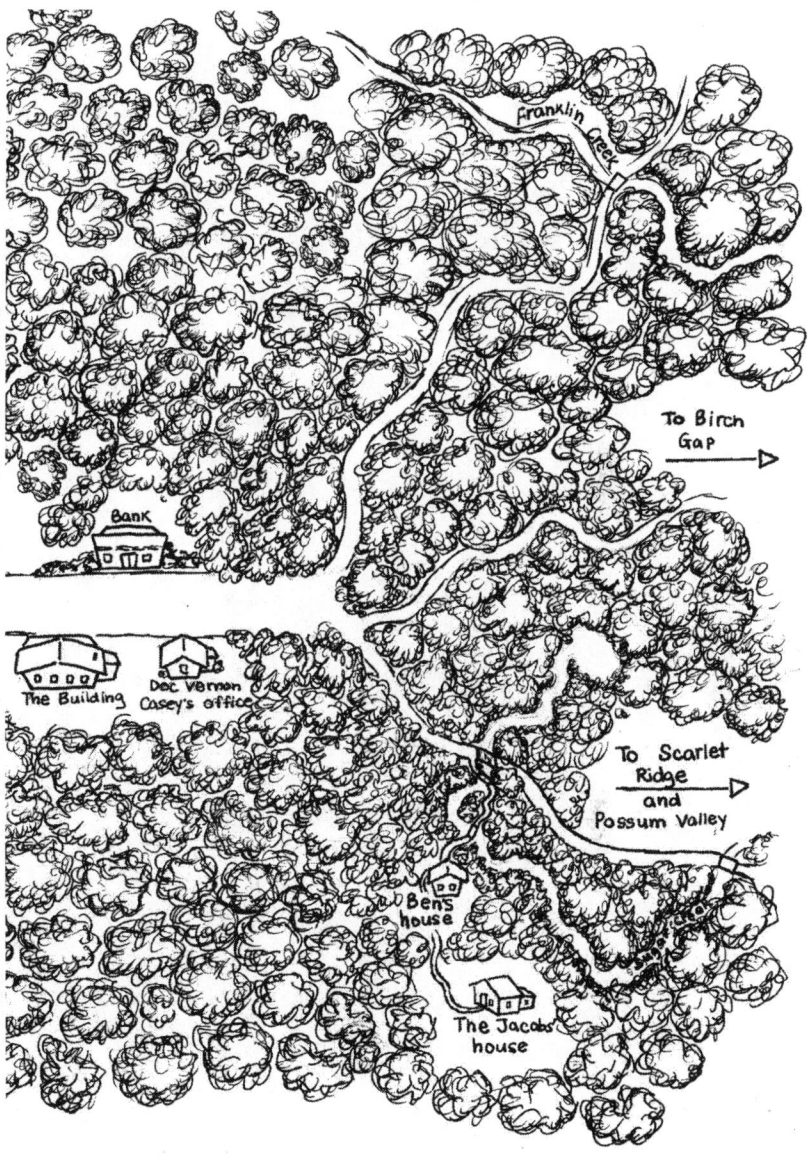

Franklin Creek

To Birch
Gap ▷

Bank

The Building

Doc Vernon
Casey's office

To Scarlet
Ridge
and
Possum Valley ▷

Ben's
house

The Jacobs
house

Other Titles by Faith Blum

I *Love* to tell the *Story*

I *Love* to tell the *Story*

Faith Blum

eBook Edition
August 2020

Cover by Amanda Tero | amandatero.com
Layout: Amanda Tero | amandatero.com
Willow Hollow map copyright 2020 by Elisabeth Grothjan,
SparrowandRoseDesigns@gmail.com

I Love to Tell the Story is a work of fiction based on historical events. All names, places, characters, and incidents are from the author's imagination. Any similarities to real people, living or dead, are entirely coincidental. All historical characters are fictionalized.

All Scriptures are paraphrased by the author from the New American Standard Bible.

*To all the pastors who have
influenced me over the years.
Thank you for always teaching
the Word of God and helping
me grow in my faith.*

Table of Contents

1

Castle City, Montana
January 1936

*L*illian wandered through the mostly deserted town. The silver boom had died long before in Castle City. Then the economic crash happened about six years ago. The only people left now were farmers and ranchers. The mountains both nearby and in the distance were the only thing keeping her here. She knew from her few travels with her father that no other part of this state compared to this area.

Beauty didn't keep everyone here, however, as was evidenced by the departure of most of the young people as soon as they came of age. All of her friends had left for bigger, and hopefully better, things. Only two girls her own age were still here in the dying town, and both of them refused to talk to her because she was friends with Rebekah Peterson. Why that mattered, Lillian had never figured out.

She sighed as she neared the Peterson house. Such a large home for a small family, but Mr. and Mrs. Peterson had planned to have a lot of children when they married, not knowing that God had other plans. Including the death of one son in the Great War and two others in infancy.

Now if she could only figure out what God's plans were for her. Her father's farm needed only one person to run it, and their small cabin took very little time to clean. Only during canning season was she extra busy. Food for two was simple, even if she made a large, fancy meal. That left way too much time to sit around and… do what? Read? Sew? Go visiting? All of those things became monotonous after a while. And that was saying a lot since she loved to read.

Tears threatened at the back of her eyes, and she roughly swiped at her eyes in an attempt to keep them away.

"Lillian!" Mrs. Peterson's voice broke into her thoughts. "Come over here if you are not too busy."

Lillian turned her head and searched for the rotund woman. She finally saw her on the front porch and made her way over. "I was actually coming to visit you. How are you?"

Mrs. Peterson stood. "I am too young to sit around and too old to have the energy to do a lot, but am otherwise doing fine. And how are you, my dear?"

Lillian sank down and sat on one of the steps. "I don't know. I don't find enjoyment in anything. It's all so repetitive. I just don't know what more I can do right now."

Mrs. Peterson patted Lillian's shoulder. "Come inside with me. I have something to share with you." She went into the house.

Lillian took a deep breath and followed close behind, trying to keep the tears at bay. Mrs. Peterson led her into the kitchen where she went to her small desk area and picked up an envelope.

"I got this letter in the mail yesterday and I think you would find it interesting. You know I have been writing to the son of my cousin, right?"

"The one who is a pastor in Kentucky?"

Mrs. Peterson smiled. "Yes, that's the one. Well, he mentioned something in this last letter about you." She held up a hand. "Before you get all huffy, yes, I did write to him about you in general terms. He knows I have treated you like the daughter I never had and that is about all. Now listen to this part." She pulled the paper out of the envelope and unfolded it. She skimmed the letter briefly. "Ah. Here it is. 'You may have heard of the WPA librarian system the president put in place. Well, our little town is part of that system! It will be so good for the library to start reaching those who don't come to town often, if at all. Unfortunately, we do not have enough people who live in the area who can be librarians. When our current librarian mentioned this to me, I immediately thought of Miss Lillian. Would you mind talking to her and asking if she would be interested in such a job? She would be most welcome to live with us at least until she is settled in. If she desires a place of her own after that time, we can help her find something.'"

Mrs. Peterson stopped and looked at Lillian.

Lillian swallowed hard. "A librarian?"

Mrs. Peterson nodded. "But it's more than that. I read an article in the newspaper about it. You would go around on horseback and bring books to people who live in the mountains."

Lillian swallowed again and forced herself to take even breaths. This sounded like just what she needed. She could still read, help others who loved to read, and break up the monotony of her life here. "I will talk to Father. I would like to do it, but I don't know what he will say."

"Of course. I expected you would need to talk to him. Tell him to come talk to me if he needs to know more about Samuel."

"I will. Thank you, Mrs. Peterson!"

Lillian paced around the small one-room cabin. The only time she stopped was when she stirred supper, and then she quickly resumed her pacing. What would her father say to her? Would he allow her to go or be the overprotective father he so often was? Ever since Mrs. Peterson told her of the possibility, the idea had grown in her. One of her desires since becoming a Christian a few years earlier was to tell others about Jesus. In this small area there was no one to talk to about Jesus who didn't already know Him. Well, there was the town drunk and a few others, but talking to them would be dangerous for a young woman.

But with this job, she could help instill the love of reading in others as well as talk to them about Jesus. Even though there was a pastor in the town she would be going from, she had heard that the people in that area were very superstitious. She could show them that there was more to Christianity than a set of rules.

Lillian paused her pacing. She could use that as part of her reasoning to her father.

Her movement took her next to the stove once more and she stirred the thick dish. What had she put in there again? She hoped it would taste okay. Her mind had been wandering while she made the food, but the two times she had tasted it, it hadn't been bad.

Where was she again? Oh yes, coming up with arguments to convince her father she could do this job and why she should do it.

Boots clomped on the front porch and Lillian stopped mid-stride. Father was home. She glanced at the clock. He was early, too. She wiped her hands on her apron and took a deep breath.

Her father opened the door and stepped inside. "Hi, Lillian. How was your day?"

Lillian smiled. Her father's burly form filled the doorway. "My day was very good. How was yours?"

Her father sighed. "Long and tiring. If farming wasn't the only sure way to make a little money during these lean times, I would quit in a heartbeat."

Lillian's smile faltered. Maybe this wouldn't be the best time to talk to him.

He took a few steps forward and took her face in his hands. "What made your smile leave so quickly, my daughter?"

Lillian fought the urge to remove her father's hands from her face. "I have something to talk to you about, but I am afraid this would be a bad time."

"Because I am in a bad mood about farming?"

Lillian nodded.

Her father chuckled. "Lillian, I'm often in a bad mood about farming, although I don't always voice it. I can be reasoned with even if I don't want to necessarily deal with certain things. What'd you want to talk about?"

Lillian motioned toward the table. "Should we sit down and start eating first?"

He gave her a slight glare, but combined with his smile, it didn't hold the slightest threat. "Are you trying to bribe me?"

Lillian giggled. "Maybe?"

"I am quite hungry, so I will allow myself to be bribed."

Lillian put the plates and spoons on the table and stopped herself just before picking up the hot pot with her bare hands. She grabbed a hot pad off the counter and then picked up the pot.

She sat in the chair next to her father, folded her hands, and closed her eyes.

"Heavenly Father," his deep, rich voice filled the small cabin, "we thank You for this day that You've provided for us and for the food You allow us to have. There are so many in want in this country right now. I feel blessed to be able to provide for my family. Thank You for this wonderful daughter who puts up with me and makes delicious food, even if it is to bribe me to listen to her. In Jesus' name. Amen."

Lillian stared at her father when he finished, but he avoided her gaze. She dished up a scoop of the thick vegetable stew onto his plate. "Enjoy your bribery food, Father."

"Thank you, Lill."

Lillian tried not to smile at the endearing nickname and failed.

They both ate in silence for a few minutes before Lillian's excitement got the better of her. "Father, Mrs. Peterson learned of a job I could get if I want it."

Her father's head popped up. "Really?"

"Yes. But there's one catch. Maybe two." Lillian waited for a response, but her father kept his eyes on her and didn't open his mouth. She cleared her throat. "It's in Kentucky."

"Kentucky? The state?"

"Is there another kind?"

He chuckled. "No, I don't suppose there is. What kind of a job is it and how did she find out about it?"

Lillian relaxed slightly. "It's a job as a librarian." She told him everything Mrs. Peterson had told her.

"It does sound like a good opportunity. Let me think about it."

Lillian ducked her head. "Yes, Father."

"Now, what would you like to do tonight?"

18

She started. "I don't know. I hadn't thought about it."

"How about a game?"

Lillian nodded. She watched her father as he got up to get the cards. She hadn't thought about him and what he would do without her. If she left, he would be alone. He would have no one to cook or clean for him. No one to play games with. No one to talk to. How could she abandon him? She couldn't. She shouldn't. She should tell him that she didn't have to go. She would stay here.

He returned carrying a book rather than cards. "I found this book of memories your mother made before you were born. I had forgotten about it. Can we read through it instead of playing a game?"

Tears sprang to her eyes. "Of course. What is it about?"

"As I recall, this was what your mother did while she was bedridden waiting for you to be born. She wrote in here every day about memories from our courtship, our wedding, marriage, and her anticipation of being a mother. If I remember correctly, I was supposed to give this to you to read someday when you were old enough."

"Can you read it to me, Father?"

He smiled. "Would you like to sit in my lap, too?"

Lillian laughed as she shook her head. "I don't think that would be very comfortable anymore. When I was a little girl…"

Her father chuckled. "Leave the food to cool off and the dishes can wait as well. Let's go read."

2

Malachi and I met in Billings on one of his many visits. I'd seen him a few times and developed the most massive crush on him. Then one day he actually talked to me. He's lucky I wasn't wearing a corset or I would have fainted dead away. We talked about the weather and the town for a while before he finally asked if he could take me to the soda fountain. I had already been there once that day, but I didn't care. I don't think he ever found out, either. Someday I hope to bring you to that soda fountain, my child, and introduce you to the wonders of modern inventions.
~ Excerpt from Carlotta Sullivan's memory journal

*J*t took Lillian hours to fall asleep. Her mind raced with everything her father had read in the journal. Her father had suggested they not read the whole thing at once, so they had stopped shortly after the wedding and only months before her older brother would be stillborn.

In the morning, Lillian cleaned up the supper dishes while she made hotcakes, sausage, and gravy. She let the dishes soak as long as she could before scrubbing them.

Her father said little during breakfast, and none of it was about her mother or the job she wanted. She bit her tongue to keep from asking him about it. He would talk to her about everything in his own time. She had learned long ago that nagging did nothing.

Lillian cooked and cleaned everything more thoroughly than she had done for months. This time, she decided to really bribe her father and made his favorite meal and dessert. Sugar was scarce, but she figured this would be as good a time as any to use some. While the pie baked, she went outside and whistled for her horse. She fed her a carrot and petted her gray nose. "Would you want to come with me, Apple?" The horse whinnied and Lillian laughed. "Of course you do. You love adventures. I wouldn't want to deny you this, but it costs extra to transport a horse by train. I don't know if Father would allow that. No matter what, I'll be sure to take you for a nice long ride before I leave. If you can come with me, I will do it so you can get one last stretch in before our long journey. I wonder how long it takes to get to Kentucky from here."

She thought about the question as she wandered slowly back to the house. She finished the pie, decorating it as best she could, and set it on the table to cool off. Now all she had to do was wait. And wait some more. She sat in the living area with a book in her lap and her crocheting, holding it open as she worked on the sweater for her father. She had started it just after Christmas the year before and it needed to be done soon. Very, very soon.

That evening, Lillian waited for her father to come in from the barn, but he didn't come. Lillian was about to remove the food from the stove when he stumbled into the back door.

"Father? Are you okay?"

Her father nodded. "Sorry. Yes. I got so caught up in what I was doing in the barn, and then when I started walking to the house, I got a bit lightheaded. I'll be fine."

Lillian rushed over to the water bucket and brought a ladleful of water to him. "Drink this."

Her father sat in the chair closest to him and drank the water. "Thank you."

She smiled and nodded. "Are you almost ready to eat?"

"Yes, please! I'm starving!"

After she put the food on the table and her father prayed, for the second time in as many days, Lillian tried hard not to ask the question deep on her mind. Her father would tell her when he was ready.

"Lillian," her father said, "this is a delicious meal. I really appreciate it. During work today, I thought a lot about this job opportunity you have. I want you to be happy and I know how hard it's been here for you. I also know that there are very few young men here, which means I have little hope of grandchildren if I don't let you fly the nest. I've decided that you can go. On one condition."

Lillian's heart jumped as her throat tightened and hands went to her chest. She breathed rapidly. "What condition?"

"That you write to me often."

Lillian laughed as her breathing became more regular. "Of course, Father. Who do you think I am? I love to write almost as much as I love to read. I will write to you every day I can." Her grin stayed on her face, unable to be wiped off.

He stood, went to his daughter, and pulled her into a tight hug. "I love you, Lillian. I always will no matter how far away you are. Come back to me someday."

Lillian put her arms as far around him as she could, barely touching her fingers together. She snuggled up against his chest, breathing in deeply. "I will, Father. I love you, too. I couldn't abandon you completely. You are the only parent I have ever known. That is something I can never forget."

They hugged each other in silence for a few minutes. Lillian was the one to finally pull away. "I have pie. Would you like some?"

Her father laughed heartily. "Have I *ever* turned down pie?"

Lillian's grin widened. "Never to my knowledge."

It took Lillian three days to prepare for her trip. She packed, unpacked, and repacked countless times as she tried to keep her things to a minimum. From what Mrs. Peterson said, the people in the Appalachians had very little, so she didn't want them to feel like she was showing off to them. In the end, she packed one good dress and two work dresses, a few books, her Bible, and the journal from her mother. She had finished reading it with her father the night before the planned departure, but wanted to have it to read through again when she thought of it.

Today, she had the hardest task of all.

Her father entered the house early. "Father! You are just the person I wanted to see."

"Of course I am. Who else would you want to see? Unless there is someone who has turned your fancy." He winked.

Lillian felt her face grow warm. "No, I haven't met anyone who could turn my fancy. At least not a human."

Her father turned a curious look to her. "Who is the non-human who turned your fancy?"

"Apple."

"Your horse?"

Lillian nodded.

"I see. And you want to bring her with you."

Lillian took a deep breath. "If that is possible, yes."

She watched her father's face, trying to read it as he stared back at her. He gave nothing away. She finally looked away and went to the kitchen area to finish supper before it burned to the pan.

"You can take her," her father said softly.

She spun around, flinging beans onto the table from the spoon. "Really? Even though it costs extra?"

Her father nodded. "You will have to find a place in town to board her and feed her from the money you earn. Are you prepared to do that?"

Lillian set the spoon down and ran to her father, hugging him tightly. "Absolutely. Thank you so much, Father! You are wonderful!"

Her father hugged her back and leaned his head down. "I know I am."

Lillian pulled back and laughed. "You're also very humble."

Her father winked and she went back to finishing supper.

3

Malachi and I courted mostly through letters for a long time since we lived so far from each other. I wrote a letter every single day. Sometimes, I even wrote more than one. I hope you get to read those letters someday, my child. I fell in love with Malachi because of his kind, gentle manner. He has always been that way and from what I hear, takes after his mother, Emily. I hope you get to meet her, although, with how sick she is, I don't know if she will survive to meet you. Your father will always do the right thing for everybody else no matter what it does to him. I love him for that. He is doing so much for me right now. I had a hard time with it at first since he shouldn't have to do so much, especially since it is my job as his wife to take care of him, the food, and the house. And now I can't do any of that. He keeps claiming he doesn't mind because he would rather have a healthy baby. I suppose that must be true, but that doesn't make it any easier. Thankfully, Mrs. Peterson comes over often to help around the house. She is such a sweet woman. I hope you get to know her as well. There are many people here I hope you get to know when you are older.
~ Excerpt from Carlotta Sullivan's memory journal

*T*he day before leaving for Bozeman to get on a train, Lillian said goodbye to the few friends she had in town. She saved the hardest for last.

"Are you ready to go?" Mrs. Peterson asked.

Lillian shrugged. "I hope so. I don't know of anything else I will need there."

27

"And what you don't have, you can purchase."

Lillian smiled slightly. "Correct." She threw her arms around Mrs. Peterson. "I'm going to miss you so much. You have been such an integral part of my life for so long that I don't know what I'll do without you."

"Oh, darling, you will be fine. Samuel has a wife whom he praises so much that I am sure you can ask her anything once you get to know her a bit better. And the town is bigger than Castle City, so hopefully you can make some friends as well. Especially among your fellow librarians. All you have to do is get out of your shell a little and put yourself forward."

Lillian shrank back. "I know. But it is scary talking to new people."

"You will have to get used to it as a librarian. You will be meeting new people on your routes as well as in the library itself."

Lillian tried to smile. "You're right, of course. I will do my best."

"I will be praying for you. Be sure to write me."

"Oh, I will," Lillian replied. "I should go before Father wonders if I got lost."

Mrs. Peterson laughed. "Goodbye, my Lillian."

"Goodbye, Mrs. Peterson."

As she walked home, she wondered if she would ever see Mrs. Peterson again. Depending on how long she lived in Kentucky, it was entirely possible she would never come back to this town in Montana again. If it even existed in the near future. The town had once been a bustling mining town, but when the mine closed down, it started to die a slow and painful death.

She took her time walking back and looked around as she did. The trees, the hills, the gray rocks that were her father's bane of farming. She would miss them all. How could she leave this familiar place? And yet, her heart skipped every time she thought of the adventure ahead of her. She was leaving home to go to a job of her own in a new state. To live with people she didn't know, but were related to her favorite person other than her father.

As the excitement grew and tamped down any dread or fear, she broke into a run to get home faster. She needed to finish packing quickly so she could leave right away in the morning.

During the horseback ride to Bozeman, her father gave her instructions for almost everything under the sun. Making sure her money lasted, how to deal with overeager suitors, what to say to whom and when, how to show appreciation for her hosts, how to behave properly even when no one else was. She was surprised he hadn't gone over which fork to use for salad and which to use for the main dish.

Lillian tried to listen as best as she could through all of his instructions and responded appropriately to each one. The detail he went into was a bit much, but she would be patient with him and allow him to work through the nervous energy he had from letting his little girl go off on her own. She was surprised he hadn't insisted on coming with her but knew it had to be because he couldn't leave the farm, even in winter. What would Kentucky be like?

"Lillian?"

She snapped her attention back to her father. "I'm sorry, Father. I was daydreaming again."

"What were you thinking about?"

"Kentucky and how it will be different from Montana."

Her father smiled. "I hear it is mountainous as well, so it may not be that much different from here."

"What about the people?"

"They are all made in God's image, so while their customs may be different, deep down they are the same as you and I."

Lillian chewed her lower lip. "What if they don't like me?"

Her father reached a hand out to her and she touched it with her fingertips. "No one could ever dislike you, Lillian. You are too kind of a person to not be liked."

Lillian tried to smile, but failed. "Are you sure?"

Her father pulled back on his reins and came to a stop. Lillian stopped Apple next to him and he put a hand on her arm. "Lillian, you are so much like your mother. You look like her with your curly dark hair, brown eyes, and infectious smile. Every time I look at you, I think of her. The only thing visible that you got from me is your height. Your mother was one head shorter than me, but you're almost as tall as I am. But I'm happiest that you got your personality from Carlotta. You are sweet, kind, gentle, and quiet just like she was. She never insisted on anything, though she never hesitated to ask for things."

"Did you give in to her as often as you do to me?" Lillian asked as tears threatened to spill from her eyes. Her father never opened up about Mother like this.

Her father laughed. "No, not quite as often, but I did give in more times than I probably should have." He sighed. "God knew she was too good to live on this earth for too long," he added in a whisper. He took a deep breath. "Come. If we don't hurry, we won't reach the train in time for you to leave."

The goodbye at the train was a quick one after dropping Apple off in the livestock car. Lillian made sure to ask if she could visit on any stops, and the conductor—a sweet older gentleman—assured her she was more than welcome to visit the livestock car whenever it was safe to. She hugged her father tightly as the conductor announced for all to go aboard.

"I love you, Father."

"I love you, too, my Lillian. Stay safe and listen to your elders."

She smiled through her tears. "Yes, Father."

She boarded the train and hurried to a window seat, opened the window, and waved to her father as hard as her arm would go. He soon became little more than a speck in the distance and then disappeared altogether. She sank back in the seat and took in the view around her inside the train car.

The train ride had very few momentous things happen. She enjoyed the scenery as it whizzed by and visited Apple at each stop. Otherwise, nothing happened and she arrived in the small town of Evergreen Ridge without incident.

At the station, she went up to a conductor. "Excuse me, sir. Do you know the way to Willow Hollow?"

The conductor looked her up and down. "I would get a place to stay the night. The bus leaves at 9:00 a.m. for Willow Hollow and beyond."

Lillian smiled. "I have a horse."

"Ah. That makes a difference. Take the road that goes south out of town and follow it until you reach the next town. That'll be Willow Hollow."

Lillian nodded. "Thank you, sir. I appreciate your assistance."

"You're welcome, Miss." He tipped his hat and scurried off to another part of the train.

Lillian headed to the livestock car, where a porter had already unloaded Apple and was waiting for her arrival. Apple whinnied when she saw Lillian approach. The young porter looked up and caught eyes with Lillian.

"You must be the horse's owner, Miss."

Lillian smiled. "What gave you that idea?"

The porter shrugged and handed the reins over to her. "Horses are smarter than people, Miss. Always have been."

"I don't disagree there. Thank you for getting her out of the car for me."

"You're welcome, Miss. Safe travels."

Lillian took a deep breath, put her bags over Apple's back, put her saddle on, and led her through the town. She didn't want to mount her until she had seen the town a bit. She passed a building that said "Sheriff's Office" and paused. Did she trust the conductor's directions and her own sense of direction well enough? No. Especially not the latter. She tied the reins to the hitching post outside the office and went inside.

A portly gentleman with wire-rim glasses and a shiny silver star on his chest sat behind a desk to her right when she stepped through the door. The door shut with a click and the man looked up. When he saw her, he stood.

"Can I help you, Miss?"

Lillian nodded. "I am looking for directions, sir. I need to get to Willow Hollow. Would I get there before dark if I leave now?"

The sheriff came around to the front of his desk. "Yes, ma'am. You can ride there easily in two hours. As for how to

32

get there, just take this road that way"—he pointed to his right—"and you'll get there with no trouble as long as you don't leave the road."

Lillian held out her hand and he shook it. "Thank you for your help."

"May I ask what business you have in Willow Hollow?"

"I am going to become a librarian." The sheriff's bushy eyebrows rose slightly and she smiled. "Thank you again, sir."

"You're most welcome. Safe travels."

4

I know most women say this, but our wedding day was magical. I cannot describe how wonderful it was. The weather couldn't have been more perfect. Assuming you have lived in Montana most of your life, you know how rare that is. It wasn't too hot or too cold. The sun shone with just a few wispy clouds in it. Oh my darling baby, I wish there had been a way to capture how beautiful the day was. We had simple vows that we wrote ourselves and then we celebrated with our friends and family. Our mothers and sisters made the food for the wedding with help from a few others. I don't even remember what I ate. I was too in love and overwhelmed by what I had just done to really notice. I was married! That night, I would be going home with the love of my life to live with him until death parted us. And now soon, I will be a mother.
~ Excerpt from Carlotta Sullivan's memory journal

The sky grew suddenly dark shortly after she left Evergreen Ridge. She debated turning around and staying the night in the larger town, but had telegrammed Pastor Stuart already and told him she would be arriving that day. How bad could the storm be, anyway?

Lillian enjoyed the scenery. It looked much the same as Montana with the tree-covered mountains and deep valleys. The only difference was that she had seen very few prairie-like places. Montana had many wide open spaces. Kentucky so far seemed much closer together.

Out of nowhere, a torrential downpour started and within seconds, Lillian was soaked to the skin. She groaned but kept going. Apple slowed some as the dirt road became a mud road. Lillian kept her head down to keep the water out of her eyes. As the rain showed no sign of letting up, she sighed. So much for making a good first impression. She would be coming in with dripping, straight hair and soaked clothing. Would they even let her in the house?

She couldn't think that way. Of course they would let her in and warm her up and dry her off as quickly as possible. Thunder rumbled in the distance and Lillian closed her eyes briefly. *God, keep me safe, please.*

Lightning flashed, showing her the crest of the hill Apple currently climbed, and a large crack of thunder made Apple and Lillian jump simultaneously. They reached the top of the hill. Between the dark caused by the clouds and the heavy rain, Lillian couldn't see in front of her. She heard another rumble. It sounded like thunder, but different. She thought nothing of it, though. Apple whinnied as she kept thinking about the sound. Thunder could have an odd sound once in a while, especially in the mountains. That had to be it. Although, it rarely lasted this—

Crash!

That was no thunder. Lillian looked around frantically. What was it? A horse whinnied to her left and Lillian nearly jumped out of her dress. There was another horse. She searched to her left and saw the barebacked horse hooked up to a harness. "Oh no," she muttered. She slid off of Apple and, keeping a tight hold on the reins, followed the harness lines to the small cart. The cart had tipped over, but the owner wasn't in sight.

36

A tortured groan led her around to the other side of the cart. A man lay there with only his head showing above the cart. Lillian dropped to her knees next to him. "Sir, can you hear me? God, help me help this man."

"Shut up, girl," the man growled. "Get this cart off of me."

Lillian's breath came in short gasps, but she quickly concentrated on taking deep, even breaths. Panicking would not help her or the man. Get the cart off. Right. But how? Something tugged on her hand and she looked over at Apple. A slight smile crept onto her face. Apple had pulled things before. If she hooked Apple to the other side of the cart somehow... Yes. This might just work.

She found some rope on the ground near the man's cart and found a knothole in the side to tie one end to. She tied the other part of the rope like a harness on Apple and led her toward the other side of the road. Lillian tried to help but in the end was unable to do much. The cart moved slowly, but it did move, and after she led Apple almost into the woods on the side of the road, it finally righted itself.

Lillian left Apple tied up and hurried to the man. "Can you move?"

The man shifted slightly and groaned again. "No."

Lillian bit her lip and looked around. The man was older and frail, so he might not be too heavy, but the water and mud on him made him too heavy for her. She also had to figure out a way to get him into the cart without hurting him more. "Sir?"

"What?"

"I need to get you in the cart, but I don't know how. I don't suppose you have any ideas."

The man was quiet for a minute and Lillian wondered if he had lost consciousness. "Make a travois."

"What is that?"

37

"Sled…made of branches. Two big ones for sides…ropes to tie branches across."

"How do I get you on it?"

"Walk you through…when finished." His breath came in short gasps and at the end of his sentence, he coughed lightly as if it hurt to do so.

Lillian nodded and hurried into the woods to find the supplies. She had no idea how much time passed as she made the travois. The storm had lessened by the time she finished it and dragged it back to where she had left the man. She laid the travois on the ground next to him and touched his arm. He flinched and groaned.

"Don't scare me," he growled.

"I didn't mean to," Lillian replied. "I'm sorry. We need to get you on the travois."

The man turned his head her way and looked from her to the travois. "Put it next to me on the other side and pull me onto it."

"Yes, sir," Lillian said with more confidence than she felt. She hurriedly brought the travois to the other side and took hold of his arm and leg. With considerable effort, she managed to get him on the travois and prayed it stayed together.

"What is your name?" she asked.

"Why?"

"I thought it would make conversing easier if I knew your name."

The man huffed. "Women. I'm Crow. But no talking."

Lillian held out a hand. "I'm Lillian, Mr. Crow. I'm sorry we had to meet this way. I'll go hook you up to a horse and we'll be on our way in no time." She left him again, letting out a long breath as she did. She didn't like to talk, but she couldn't stand this silence either. Sometime during the making of the travois, the rain had stopped and now the only noises were her movements, the horses, and the occasional groan from Mr. Crow. Not a bird made a sound. She hoped that didn't mean the storm was about to get worse. That was the last thing they needed. She untied Apple from the side of the cart and led him over to the travois. Using the rope, she tied the travois to Apple's saddle and then led Mr. Crow's horse and cart in front of her and tied Crow's horse to the back of the travois. They would make a very interesting sight coming into town, but it was the best she could do.

Lillian mounted Apple and started on the long trek to town. She sneaked looks behind her as often as she dared to make sure Mr. Crow was still on his travois, but she needn't have worried. Her creation was sturdy enough, and Apple was a gentle horse even though she wasn't used to pulling things often. Rain began to sprinkle on them as they approached the edge of the small town.

Through the mist, she was able to see the drab buildings from the top of the small hill. She went down the slope carefully and as she entered the town, she tried to find a sign for the doctor's office. No one was outside at all. The town seemed haunted and deserted. If she hadn't been told that the first town on this road was Willow Hollow, she would have ridden right through it without hesitation. She rode past the blacksmith shop, the general store, the church, and another big building before finally spotting the doctor's shingle on the door of the last building on the right. Now to hope he was in his office and not out on a call somewhere.

Lillian hopped off the cart and ran to the door, pounding on it with her fist as soon as she got close enough.

"I'm coming, I'm coming," a voice from inside said. "Have a little patience. I know you probably think things are a matter of life and death, but they aren't always, so give me a little time to make it to the door."

The door opened and the first word that came to Lillian's mind was *hawk*. His nose looked like a hawk's beak. He was also quite tall. She only came up to his shoulders.

"What do you need, young lady?" the doctor asked, peering at her with his dark eyes.

Lillian swallowed. "There's an old man that needs your help. His cart overturned on top of him."

The doctor followed Lillian to the travois and did a quick examination before untying the travois from Apple and pulling it inside the office. Lillian tied the man's horse to the hitching post and hurried in after the doctor.

"Good. You came in," the doctor said absently. "Help me get him onto the bed here. You take his feet."

Lillian did as ordered and hovered nearby as the doctor finished his examination.

"Crow is lucky you came by when you did," the doctor said.

Lillian winced. "I think my horse may have been the one to cause the cart to overturn, actually. The dark and rain made it too hard to see, and I think my horse's whinny scared his horse and caused it to overturn onto him."

"Hmm," the doctor muttered. "That's possible. I have told this old fool many times he needs a new horse. That old nag is too unstable to pull his cart anymore. She had bad energy coming from her. But will he listen? No, of course not." He looked up at her. "We haven't met. I am Dr. Vernon Casey."

Lillian tried to smile. "Lillian Sullivan. I am coming to be a horseback librarian."

"Ah, yes. I heard someone was coming for that. Are you the one who plans to stay with the pastor's family?"

"Yes, Dr. Casey, that's correct."

"You're a brave young woman."

"Why do you say that?"

Dr. Casey kept his attention on his patient as he spoke. "Pastor Stuart is a kind man, but he is very religious. He has turned many here against him by denouncing their beliefs as superstitions."

"Are you one of those people?"

Dr. Casey looked up at her. "Why do you ask?"

Lillian licked her lips and shrank back. "You mentioned Mr. Crow's horse has bad energy coming from her. That could be considered a superstition."

Dr. Casey didn't respond and Lillian let the conversation drop. She wasn't bold enough to say more anyway. "Will he survive?"

"I don't know yet. His injuries are worse than I thought they would be. I don't need your help anymore. Pastor Stuart is probably getting anxious about you. Bring Crow's horse with you. The pastor runs the livery and will put the horse up."

Lillian nodded before realizing Dr. Casey couldn't see her. "Yes, sir. I'll be back in the morning to check on him."

Dr. Casey didn't respond except with a muttered sound she couldn't discern.

5

Oh my dear child. I love you so. But it is also so hard to stay positive. You are my second child. My first was a son, but he was born too early and did not live long after his birth. Let me go back a little.

It was about three years after your father and I married. We were so happy together, but also desperately wanted children. When I realized I was expecting, I was ecstatic! I told Malachi as soon as the doctor confirmed it, and we started planning. We had the house ready for a baby before I even started showing. We were quite funny, actually. Then about three months before the baby was supposed to be born, I started to have intense cramping. I was in terrible pain but was also in the house all by myself. I didn't know what to do. I waited. I prayed. Finally, Malachi came in during one of my worst cramps and heard me crying. He rushed into the bedroom and told me not to worry, he would go get the doctor.

When the doctor arrived, he said there was nothing he could do. The baby was coming whether I wanted it to or not. It took all that day and into the next, but your brother was born. I got to hold him for all of his living moments and he died in my arms. Malachi was there right beside me and we prayed over him. It was such a bittersweet time.

I was bedridden for over a week by the doctor's orders. He wanted to make sure I didn't overdo it. I was fine with it. I didn't want to leave the bed, anyway. I grieved for your brother for years. It took us another three years to get pregnant again and now you have officially made it inside of me longer than your brother did. The doctor said that as long as you stay in there for three more weeks, you will have an excellent chance of surviving.

~ Excerpt from Carlotta Sullivan's memory journal

*L*illian let herself out of the office. The rain had stopped and she took a deep breath. The air smelled like home. Clean, fresh, and full of pine. But smelling the air wasn't what she should be doing. She had a family to meet. She untied the horses from the hitching post and led them down the street where she had come into town. She had barely registered that she had passed a livery right at the edge of town and headed that direction.

As she passed the church and went along in front of a house, the door flung open and a man bounded out. "Miss Sullivan, is that you?"

Lillian stopped, her stomach clenching. "Yes, it is."

The man stopped in front of her. "I am Samuel Stuart. Here, let me take the horses for you. Let's get the animals settled into the livery and then we can go into the house and get you dry. I was so worried about you when the storm came up. I wasn't sure if you were coming today or tomorrow. How was the trip?"

Lillian tried to keep up with all the fast words Pastor Stuart spewed out of his mouth. "The trip was almost uneventful except for the storm."

"Did you bring this travois?"

"Yes." She explained what had happened while she and the pastor unhooked the horses, brushed them down, and got them into stalls.

"Now to get you taken care of. I'm sure Crow is in good hands with the doctor, so don't worry about him at all."

"The doctor doesn't seem to like you."

"Few people around here do, but we manage anyway. The mountain people are superstitious and set in their ways. God doesn't always fit into their lives like He should. But enough

44

about that. Come. Let's go introduce you to my family, and then Patience will draw you a bath to warm you up."

Lillian smiled. "Thank you. I would appreciate that."

Lillian followed the tall, thin man out of the livery stable, to the left, and into a small clapboard house situated between the livery and the church. As she stepped through the door, she instantly felt at home. The house was very similar to her father's back in Montana, and the smell of bread reminded her of walking into Mrs. Peterson's house. A smile flitted on her face.

"Patience, this is Lillian, the young lady my cousin has befriended," Pastor Stuart said.

A beautiful woman with wavy auburn hair and brilliant green eyes stepped forward with both arms outstretched. She gave Lillian a quick hug, to which Lillian responded with an uncomfortable return to the hug. "I'm so glad you made it safely. We were so worried about you when the storm hit. Come. I have a hot bath being prepared right now. Where are your bags? We should check the clothes in them to make sure they are still dry. If not, you can wear some of mine." Patience looked her up and down. "They would be a little large for you, but would work well enough for a short time."

Lillian's mouth went dry. Pastor and Mrs. Stuart were so outgoing and talked so much. She wasn't used to having more than one person like that around at a time. "I think my bags are still attached to the saddle. I forgot about them—"

"Jed!" Patience said in a slightly louder voice.

A thin young man who looked to be around thirteen with unruly red hair bounded in from another room. "Yes, Ma?"

"Lillian left her bags attached to her saddle in the livery. Go get them for her, please."

Jed stepped forward and held out a hand. "I'm Jed. It's nice to meet you, Miss Lillian."

Lillian's smile returned briefly as she shook his hand. "It is nice to meet you as well."

Jed left and his absence revealed two young girls who had been hiding behind him. The older of the two tried to scurry away, but her mother stopped her.

"Abigail, Mary, this is Miss Lillian. She will be staying with us." Patience turned to Lillian. "Lillian, this is Abigail, my eldest daughter, who is eleven, and Mary, our youngest at seven, at least for a short time." Patience patted her swollen abdomen.

"It is a pleasure to meet you both," Lillian said.

"All right, you two may go now," Patience said.

Abigail left without even the whisper of a sound, but Mary stayed and looked up at Lillian with a questioning look on her face.

"Do you need something, Mary?" Patience asked.

"No."

"Then go play with your sister, please."

"Abigail only wants to read," Mary answered.

Patience sighed. "Excuse me a moment, Lillian. The bath is in the kitchen with more hot water heating on the stove. If you would like, you can check the temperature and add more water to it. I'll be in there soon to help you finish getting everything ready."

Lillian nodded, but Patience didn't see it as she turned her attention to her daughter. Lillian didn't mind. From the quick introductions she had gotten, it appeared she had most in common with Abigail. What she wouldn't do to be in a room all by herself with a book to read. *Later*, she thought. *I can read later.* She found the kitchen and checked the bath water. It was almost hot enough and probably also full enough. She hoped her clothes in her bag had stayed somewhat dry during the trip and all of the rain it had gotten the last few hours.

She found the water on the stove, and next to the stove were two towels that looked like they had been used earlier to pick up the hot pan. Lillian put a hand just over top of the water. It was steaming enough to feel pretty warm. Between that and the bubbles forming on the sides and bottom of the pan, she knew it was getting close to boiling. She decided to let it heat up a little more before dumping it in the tub.

Before the water got hot enough, Patience was back.

"I'm terribly sorry about that. Abigail loves to read and that upsets Mary because she doesn't like to read. She would rather be outside working or playing. Or even inside playing something fun and that doesn't require strategy. Is there anything you need?"

A knock sounded on the door to the kitchen.

"Come in," Patience said.

Jed stepped in carrying Lillian's bags. "I didn't know if everyone was decent." He set the bags on the floor. "Here are your bags, Miss Lillian."

"Thank you, Jed," Lillian answered. "I appreciate it." She knelt to start going through the bags, and Mrs. Stuart joined her as Jed left the room and closed the door.

"It appears most of this stayed dry. I am surprised."

Lillian smiled. "Father's idea must have worked."

"And what idea was that?"

Lillian pointed to the inside of the bag. "Father lined all the bags with leather to help them stay dry."

"Your pa is a smart man. Well, I will leave you to your bath now. After I add the hot water for you."

"I can do that," Lillian protested. "You shouldn't lift heavy pans in your condition."

"I insist." Patience reached the stove before Lillian could do anything about it, and she stood back and began unbuttoning her dress.

"Thank you for your help, Mrs. Stuart."

"You're welcome. Just holler if you need anything. This house isn't too big, so I can hear you from pretty much everywhere."

Lillian smiled as Patience left the room.

She was alone. In a strange kitchen about to take a bath. No one would walk in, right? She had to trust that they wouldn't. She slipped into the tub and breathed a sigh of contentment. Beautiful, warm water. It warmed her up, too, which she needed after the chill of the rain had soaked into her. She let herself soak for a few minutes before taking the bar of soap Patience had left nearby and scrubbed herself and her hair.

By the time she finished, the water was a murky brown. Not as bad as she had seen after her father's baths, but still bad. She shuddered at the thought of having so much dirt on her. A towel hung on the back of a nearby chair and she reached for it as she stood. She dried off everything except her hair, saving that for last as always. Then she worked on her hair. Even with the shorter haircut she had now, it still seemed to take forever to dry. Probably because it was thick hair. She finally got it as dry as possible with a towel and then hurriedly dressed.

6

My dear child, I hope this section hasn't been too sad for you, but I needed to get it out. I pray for you every day. I can't bear the thought of losing another child. You are everything to me right now. Of course, God and my husband are, too. But I think if you have lost a child and then get pregnant again, you have a little fear that this child will not survive either. I don't know if I can go through all of that pain again. But on with the story a bit more. The funeral for your brother was one of the hardest things I have ever had to go through. The coffin was so small. No one should ever have to be buried in such a tiny wooden box. Before he was buried, I took one last look at his perfect little face. Then he was lowered into the grave and buried in dirt. If I wasn't bedridden, I would go visit him once a week as I did after he was born. Every Sunday, it became a ritual. We would go to church, come home and eat lunch, and then Malachi and I would take a walk out to his grave. I can't tell you how many times I cried every day. After a while, it got better and I didn't cry as much or as often. When I started getting the feeling I was expecting you, little one, I'm afraid my excitement was a little less than with your brother. I was apprehensive at first. But the doctor assured me that he would keep a close eye on both of us and so far, everything is going well.
God helped me through my grief. If you ever go through hard times, my child, turn to God and He will always help you.
~ Excerpt from Carlotta Sullivan's memory journal

$\mathcal{A}$fter a fun night getting to know the Stuart family and talking to Abigail about some of her favorite books, Lillian went to bed. In the morning, she got up at the crack of dawn as always and found Patience in the kitchen already.

"Good morning, Mrs. Stuart."

"Good morning, Lillian. Did you sleep well?"

Lillian smiled. "Yes, thank you. I think you make your mattresses the same way I do. It felt exactly like the one I have in my room at home."

Patience laughed. "There aren't very many ways to make your own mattress, so unless we were to buy a mattress, they should all be about the same."

"True. Can I help with anything?"

"Sure. Would you like to make the biscuits for breakfast?"

"I'd love to."

They worked together, chatting all the while until the children traipsed down the stairs and joined them. Then Mary and Jed took up most of the conversation as they quizzed Lillian on everything from how she slept to what she thought of their breakfast to her thoughts on what the Bible said about numerous topics.

"All right, chill'ens," Patience said. "Enough pesterin' of our guest. Jed, go out and see if your father needs help in the livery and then tell him breakfast is ready. Abigail and Mary, set the table. Lillian, could you please check the biscuits in the oven?"

"Yes, ma'am."

While they ate, Pastor Stuart asked if she would like to meet the head librarian.

"Yes, please. But can we stop at the doctor's office first?"

"Of course," Pastor Stuart said. "Are you feeling okay?"

Lillian nodded. "Yes. I am fine, but Crow may not be and I want to check on him."

"Oh yes. You said it was Crow Williams, correct?"

"Yes."

Pastor Stuart stroked his chin. "I wouldn't mind checking in on him, too. We'll start there and then I'll introduce you to Curt."

"Thank you."

When they finished eating, Lillian tried to help clean off the table, but Patience shooed her away. "Go run your errands. I have two daughters who can help me."

Lillian smiled. "Thank you, Mrs. Stuart." She went upstairs to her room, grabbed her shawl, and came downstairs to find Pastor Stuart waiting for her.

"Ready?"

"I hope so."

Pastor Stuart put a hand on her shoulder and squeezed it lightly. "You'll do fine."

They stepped outside and Lillian breathed in deep. The air had a nippy bite to it and a fresh, clean smell. "I've always loved the smell right after rain. But I have never experienced it in February."

Pastor Stuart guffawed. "You are no longer in Montana, Lillian. Kentucky has very different weather than you are used to."

"I know. But I still thought you would have some snow here."

"We do get snow once in a while, but it doesn't usually stay for long." He stopped in front of the doctor's office and knocked on the door.

"Come in," the doctor's muffled voice came through the door.

They entered the office.

"Keep coming. If you're here to see Crow, he's back here with me and insisting on going home."

"That's a good thing, right?" Lillian whispered.

Pastor Stuart shrugged. "With Crow Williams, it could mean anything. He's a persnickety old man who will do anything to get his own way. Come." He led the way into the room to the right.

The doctor leaned over the frail body of Mr. Williams.

"Is he okay?" Lillian asked.

"He had a cart fall on him," the doctor said. "Of course he's not okay. But he's doing better than I would have expected." He straightened and walked past them, beckoning for them to follow. Once they left the room, he closed the door. "I don't think he is going to survive. He's an old man with brittle bones and he got drenched in the cold rain as well. If the bone crushing doesn't kill him, the probable pneumonia will."

Lillian put a hand to her mouth. "Are you sure?"

The doctor looked at her. "Of course I'm sure. I know my work. Sometimes too well."

Lillian bit her lip. "Is there anything I can do?"

"Try to convince him to not go home. It isn't safe to move him, but I think he knows that he is going to die and wants to die at home rather than here."

Lillian nodded. "I'll try." She went into the room and approached the bed. "Mr. Williams? How are you feeling this morning?"

"Miserable," the man said. "Why're you here?"

"I came to see how you are and see if I can help."

"I wanna go home. I don't need this quack of a doc hoverin' over me all the time. If I'm gonna die, I wanna die at home."

Lillian's heart clenched. She needed to share God with him. But how could she do that when he had every reason to hate her for being the cause of his cart overturning? And he obviously didn't want to hear anything like that today. Maybe another day. "The doctor thinks you will be more comfortable here, and if you are here, you can get the care you need when you need it."

"I don't want to stay here. I don't need to be comfortable here. I can be more comfortable at home and I can take care of myself over there."

A man grunted behind her and she spun around to find the doctor standing there. "Very well, I'll make arrangements for you to get home. You may leave now, Miss Sullivan."

Lillian put a hand on top of Mr. Williams'. "Take care of yourself and I will come out to visit you as soon as I can."

"Don't bother. I'll probably be dead in a few days anyway."

Lillian left before her tears could do anything more than threaten to fall out of her eyes. As soon as she saw the pastor, she said, "Let's go to the library before I start bawling and make a spectacle of myself."

Pastor Stuart smiled. "Yes, ma'am."

7

It took me a while, but I moved on from my grief. I threw myself into my housework and kept the house spotless. When I didn't have anything to do, I would read. I read my Bible, books, and anything I could get my hands on. My child, I hope you learn to love books as much as I do. If not, I don't know what I shall do. Malachi is home. I'll continue on soon.
~ *Excerpt from Carlotta Sullivan's memory journal*

$\mathcal{P}$astor Stuart led the way to the biggest building in the town and entered the front door without knocking.

"You can just walk in?"

Pastor Stuart chuckled. "Yes, you can. This is a public building and houses the library and a few other spaces."

Lillian's eyes brightened. "Where's the library?"

"Patience, Miss Sullivan. You will see the library when you see Curt."

"And Curt is?"

"The head librarian."

"He also likes to talk about himself rather than be talked about," a new voice said.

Lillian turned and saw a thin man not much taller than herself wearing a suit. His smile put her at ease instantly. "I'm Lillian Sullivan."

"You are a long way from home; that is, it's a pleasure to meet you, Miss Sullivan."

Lillian smiled. "Yes, but I needed the change."

"Come. Let's go to my office and talk." Curt beckoned to her to follow.

"I'll leave you in Curt's capable hands," Pastor Stuart said.

"Oh yes, I'm sorry, Pastor. I forgot you were there. It is good to see you. Thank you for taking Miss Sullivan in. All of the rooms either have been let out here or will be soon."

"Patience and I have always wanted to have more people living with us. You know how hospitable she is."

Curt's laugh filled the room. "I do know. I'll see you in church, Pastor."

"I'll count on it."

Lillian waited until Curt turned back to face her.

"Shall we go?"

Lillian nodded.

"How was your trip to Kentucky?"

Lillian took a deep breath and told him of all her adventures. "I feel so bad for Mr. Williams. He had no idea I was there and now he is dying because of me."

"Not because of you, my dear. He would be dead already if it weren't for you. You did everything you could. Besides, everyone knows that Mr. Williams' horse is the most skittish one in town and that his cart has never been the most steady conveyance. It was only a matter of time before the horse made his cart upset. He is lucky it happened when it did so you could help him, or he would have died in agony and alone."

Lillian followed Curt into a large room in the building and sat in the nearest chair. "Thank you. I still feel bad about it, though."

"Then feel free to spend some time with him. Perhaps you can read a few books to him. He probably won't like it at first, but you can always give it a try."

Lillian smiled. "I might just do that. We should get down to business, though. What would you like me to do here?"

"You will be expected to take the Birch Gap route to deliver books. We also have a monthly meeting here. But most of the time, you'll be bringing books to the people who live up in the mountains. I'll ride with you the first time since you're new here, but after that you'll be on your own. That is, you shouldn't need my help. It'd be helpful for you to memorize the names of the people along your route, but it may take a few trips."

Lillian chewed her lower lip. "What do you do in bad weather?"

"An excellent question. You can check in here to see if there's any work to be done and continue your routes the next day. I believe in the case of a thunderstorm, you would help here at the library and continue your routes the next day."

Lillian nodded. "This all sounds good to me. When do I start?"

Curt chuckled. "Eager to get started already. I like that. You will start Monday."

"Perfect. What do I need to know?"

"As I said, I will take you on your routes at first to introduce you to the people as well as show you the paths to take. Then the week after I do that, you will be expected to do it yourself. Another thing is that the people will likely be suspicious of you for a while. They have even been suspicious of Lena and she has lived in Willow Hollow her whole life."

"Will they warm up to me eventually?"

"They should."

57

"Good. Thanks. Anything else?"

Curt tapped his chin. "I don't think so. Would you like to take a tour of the library?"

Lillian grinned. "I'd love to."

*Malachi and I wanted as many children as possible, so as soon as it
was safe, we tried again. I don't know what God was doing to us. I
don't think we will ever know. All I wanted was for my empty arms to be
filled. And it wasn't happening. Women at church were getting pregnant
almost as soon as they had their babies. It wasn't fair. My friends who
didn't even care if they had children were getting pregnant.
Every time I saw a baby, I would feel the pit of jealousy welling up in
me. At first, I tried to squash it, knowing it was wrong of me. But there
were times I simply could not. Then came the blessed time when I began
to feel sick. No one I knew had the flu, so I prayed so hard that my
sickness was not catching. When it lasted longer than a week, I went to
the doctor, and he confirmed what I already suspected. I was pregnant
with you! We set up a few things to do differently this time. I would take
it easy as much as possible and if anything ever seemed off, I would see
him to make sure you were okay. So far, nothing like that has happened
except this extended bed rest. But I do not mind at all. If it means I get
to see your little face and hold you to my bosom, I will count myself
among the most blessed of women.*
~ Excerpt from Carlotta Sullivan's memory journal

*A*s she walked into the churchyard with Patience Stuart on
Sunday morning, Lillian suddenly hung back. There were so
many people milling around the yard talking to one another. It
had to be at least twice the number of people that went to their
small church in Castle City. Where had they all come from?
Surely they didn't all live in town. She had heard of the

superstitions of the mountain people and figured the church would be struggling to survive, not thriving.

"Lillian. Come meet some of the people here," Patience called to her.

Lillian hurried to catch up to her and got introduced around. As the bell rang, she noticed a thin wisp of a girl on the outskirts of the crowd. "Who is that?"

Patience looked around. "Who?"

"The girl standing off to the side by herself."

"Oh, that is Lena Davis. She is the other librarian who will be working with you. She is a shy girl who adores books. I don't know her very well, but she seems very nice. I think you'd like her."

They kept walking into the church as Lillian whispered to Patience, "I hope so. I would like to have a friend my age. How old is she?"

"I believe she is sixteen, so about two years younger than you."

Lillian smiled as they sat in a wooden pew near the front where the Stuart children were already settled in. She sat through the service, comparing it to the ones she was used to. So much was the same, but even though Pastor Stuart and her pastor were distant cousins, their styles were very different. She liked it.

After the service, Lillian tried to find Lena and introduce herself, but she was nowhere to be found. She sighed and promised herself to be at the Building early enough to catch her before she went on her route.

Later that afternoon, Lillian approached Pastor and Mrs. Stuart. "Do you think it would be all right for me to go visit Crow Williams and see how he is doing?"

Patience looked over at her husband, who stroked his clean-shaven chin. "I reckon that would be fine," he responded. "Make sure you are back before dark, though."

"Thank you," Lillian said with a smile. "Where does he live?"

"Is he back home already?" Pastor asked.

"Yes," Lillian answered. "The doctor stopped me on the way home today and told me."

"Ah. Jed?"

"Yes, Pa?"

"Can you please escort Miss Sullivan to Crow Williams' place."

Jed jumped up. "Sure."

Lillian choked down a chuckle at his enthusiasm. "I'll go get my shawl and then I will be ready."

"Yes, ma'am."

As she reached the doorway, she turned. "I'm only a few years older than you, Jed. 'Ma'am' is a bit too old sounding to me. Miss or Lillian is fine."

Jed's cheeks reddened. "Yes, Miss."

Lillian held back a smile as she went to her room to get her shawl. Jed was a sweet young man, but a bit too overeager at times. She hurried back downstairs and found Jed at the front door waiting for her. "Thank you for taking time to go with me, Jed."

"You're welcome. I'm happy to do it. I prefer being outside than inside, but Pa doesn't like me to be outside on Sundays because he thinks it should be a day of rest and I like to spend time with the horses, which he says is work. But I don't think it is. I enjoy it too much for it to be work."

"Even if you do enjoy it, working with the horses is still work. You still have to feed them and make sure they have clean water, but anything else is optional and can wait for another day."

"But I have school the other days of the week, which takes me away from them."

Lillian laughed quietly. "You'll finish school soon enough and then you'll have all the time in the world to spend with your horses."

Jed sighed dramatically. "I suppose. It's just hard to be patient."

"I know what you mean. At least you live in a town that seems to have more people than Castle City."

"Really? Why do you say that?"

"Because Castle City is becoming a ghost town. I'm afraid it will die as soon as more people my father's age die. All the young people are moving away to bigger cities where there are actually jobs to be had and people to be around. There were four people my age still living there when I left. And none of them were worth getting to know."

"Why not?"

"The two young men were lazy and spent most of their time in the saloon spending their pa's hard-earned money. The two young ladies didn't think about anything but dresses and boys and getting married. Not to say I don't want to get married. I do someday; I just don't want to talk about it nonstop like they do. And I want to talk about it more seriously and realistically than they do. They read too many romance books, and it gives them a skewed point of view on what courtship and marriage really ought to be like."

Jed was quiet for a few minutes. "We're almost there."

Lillian looked around. "I don't see any houses."

Jed grinned. "Crow lives in the middle of nowhere and has his shack hidden in the trees so people can't find him very easily."

Lillian shuddered. "I could never live this far away from people all by myself. I would be too scared."

"I think that's why Crow likes it so much."

"Probably. He does seem a bit cantankerous and like he doesn't want people around."

Jed laughed. "That's a good description of him."

"Did he ever go to your pa's church?"

"Not that I know of, but Pa started the church before I was born, so I wouldn't know for sure."

Lillian nodded.

Jed took her off the road onto a faint trail. "There's another trail up ahead further for his cart, but this one is easier to walk on and leads to the same place."

Lillian lifted her skirts to keep them from getting caught on the underbrush. "You weren't kidding when you said he lived in the middle of the trees."

"Nope."

Their talking stopped as they made their way down the trail. A couple minutes later, a clearing suddenly opened up and Lillian smiled at the sight of the old cabin.

"There it is," Jed said. "Do you want me to stay with you?"

"Thank you for the offer, but I don't think so."

"You sure you can find your way back?"

"Yes."

"Then I will leave you here."

"Thank you for bringing me."

"You're welcome."

9

My dearest child, Now I come to the part where I became bedridden. The pregnancy was about halfway to its end, and I was working just as hard as I would on a normal day. I was doing the laundry and cooking both at the same time, I believe. I had a sharp pain in my abdomen a few times, but ignored it and kept scrubbing the clothes. They needed to be done and I couldn't stop just because of a little pain. Then the pain got worse and lasted longer. That's when I started to worry. I finished all the laundry I could, took the food off the stove, and lay down. The pains came a few more times, but lessened each time. When Malachi came in for lunch, he found me in bed and I asked him to go get the doctor. I told the doctor what had happened and he asked if I could still feel you moving. You are an active little baby and I still felt you moving around inside of me, thankfully. The doctor ordered me to not do any strenuous labor such as laundry or deep cleaning. I can still sweep the floors, but not scrub them. I can also cook as long as it is simple meals that don't require me standing for too long. Rebekah Peterson comes over to help as often as she can. She is also expecting, but later than me and knows how much I need the help. She also knows the ache of my mother's heart. She lost one son to the war, and eight years ago, her daughter died of scarlet fever. Speaking of her, she just came in and I should go greet her.
~ Excerpt from Carlotta Sullivan's memory journal

Lillian approached the small shack and knocked on the door.

"Go away!" Crow Williams' voice came through the door.

"Mr. Williams, it's Lillian Sullivan. I would like to come in and make you a small meal to eat."

"Don't need your charity, girl. You've done enough."

Lillian swallowed around the lump in her throat and opened the door. "I feel responsible for you being hurt and I want to help in any way I can."

Crow Williams lay in his bed against the far wall of the small cabin. "You ain't responsible, so go."

Lillian ignored the glare he gave her and went to the fireplace. A fire already burned brightly. She rummaged around to find out what food he had in his home. Not much. It was easy to see he had lived alone for many years. His pans were coated in a layer of crust and smelled of rotting food. How could she cook him something nourishing in this filth? "Where is your water pump?"

"Don't matter."

Lillian put her hands on her hips. "And what can you do to stop me?"

Crow Williams ground his teeth. "Fine. Do what you want."

"Thank you." She went outside and filled both of his pans with water, then returned inside and put the pans over the fire. "Those need to heat up a bit. Is there anything I can do to make you more comfortable?"

"I don't reckon."

Lillian swept her eyes over the tattered quilts and sighed. "If I had the time, I'd make you a quilt so you could actually be warm. These don't do you much good."

"Ye ain't takin' m' quilts. They's the only thing I've left from my wife."

Lillian let out a long breath. "I won't take them, Mr. Williams. I didn't realize you had been married before."

"I was."

Lillian bit the inside of her lip. If they couldn't talk about his wife, what could they talk about? "Did you have any children?"

"Yes."

She smiled. "Where are they now?"

"Gone. Don't know where. They never write."

Lillian's smile fell. "Oh. I'm sorry. So we can't contact them for you."

"No."

Lillian swallowed hard. She knew she needed to tell him that despite his loved ones not being there, God loved him and he could feel that love for himself. But she couldn't. Not until she had gotten to know him better. "I should see if the water is hot enough yet."

Crow grunted but said nothing.

"We can talk while I am over there."

"Don't wanna."

"What do you do out here? Do you farm?"

"Used to. Mule died. Now I sell furs."

"What do they use them for?"

"Anythin' they want."

Lillian sighed. "Does anyone still make coonskin hats like Daniel Boone wore?"

"Dunno. I don't quiz 'em."

She heard the accusation in his voice and took a deep breath while staying quiet for a bit. What could she say after that? How did she talk to him when he clearly didn't want to talk? "What would you like to eat for your next meal?"

"Nothin'. I ain't hungry."

Lillian chewed her lip. "Even if you aren't hungry, you need to eat something. It isn't good for an injured man to go hungry. You're never going to get better if you don't. You need your strength."

"The injuries you caused."

Lillian stopped her smile before it could start. "I thought you said it wasn't my fault."

"It weren't. But that don't mean you didn't cause the injuries."

"Okay. I'm going to go check the temperature of the water in the pans and then work on making you a little something to eat."

Lillian didn't try to talk while she scrubbed the pans and tried to come up with an idea for a meal. She knew he wouldn't want to talk anyway, and she had run out of things to say. As she scrubbed, she stared at the few items of food he had in the house. A can of some sort of preserves, flour, sugar, dried beans, corn, and a couple eggs. Hopefully, the eggs weren't too old.

After the pans were relatively clean, she heated up some more water in one of the pans and got the beans cooking. Then she tested the eggs to see if they were rotten. The doctor or someone else must have brought them for him, because they sank straight to the bottom of the pan. She smiled and got some unleavened bread started. It would have to be unleavened because she had no yeast or sourdough starter. Hopefully, putting an egg in the dough would help it rise some, but she wasn't going to count on it. Maybe some biscuits would be better. Except there was no butter. She sighed. This could be a rather boring meal, but at least it would be something for him to eat.

Half an hour later, everything was cooking satisfactorily. Lillian brought some tea over to Mr. Williams and sat on the chair she had set there before getting the food finished. "Here. Drink this."

"No."

"It's tea, not poison. It will hydrate you and possibly help you feel a little better as well."

"I don't have tea."

Lillian smiled. "I found some peppermint leaves outside and made them into a tea for you. I have always loved peppermint tea."

Crow scowled. "Then you drink it."

Lillian picked up a second cup. "I am. I'll drink it with you."

Mr. Williams glared at her and grumbled under his breath. "Fine." He struggled to push himself into a sitting position with his one good arm and soon fell back with a tortured groan.

"Let me help you." Lillian stood and helped him prop the pillows up and lean against them. She handed the cup to him and he took a tentative sip.

"Why is it sweet?" he asked.

"Because I added a touch of honey to it."

Mr. Williams huffed. "Drink yours."

Lillian fought a smile. "Yes, sir." She took a long sip and sighed contentedly. "I think my mama got me to love peppermint tea. She said she drank it a lot when she was pregnant with me."

"Why aren't you with her now, then, instead of harassing us here in Willow Hollow?"

Lillian took another sip of her tea. "Because Mama died giving birth to me."

"Oh." He paused. "Is something burning?"

Lillian jumped up and hurried over to the stove. She shook her head as she approached. He had tricked her into leaving his side and having to respond. Maybe he wasn't so bad after all. Maybe he just didn't know how to interact with people well, especially when they said something like she had. He just hid it under a gruff exterior so no one would know what was going on inside of him.

She stirred the beans and checked the bread. It had risen ever so slightly. Now all she had to do was figure out what to do while it finished baking. Maybe he would be willing to talk about his wife. Speaking of which, she should find out if she could open the jar of preserves. She picked it up and carried it over to the bed.

"I'm making bread."

"I can smell it."

"Yes, sir. You don't have any butter, so I was wondering if we could use these preserves."

"No. No one is going to ever open that jar."

Lillian nodded. "Okay. I'll put it back." She turned and started walking toward the shelf. A quiet voice stopped her.

"Thank you."

"You're welcome," she replied without turning.

At the shelf, she set the jar down and took a deep breath. This had to have been the last preserves his wife had made for him. They probably weren't any good anymore. Too bad he wouldn't talk about her. Lillian would have loved to hear stories.

"Do you read books?" The words flew out of her mouth without her permission.

Mr. Williams grumbled. "No. I can't."

"Oh. Perhaps I could bring a book over here next time I come and read it out loud to you. My father used to do that all the time for me. I loved hearing him read."

"Is he dead, too?"

"No," Lillian said, returning to her chair. "He is still alive and taking care of his farm."

"Why aren't you with him?"

"I wanted something new to do, and Father has always been supportive of me and agreed to let me come here."

"No father should let their daughter travel alone. Where are you from?"

"Montana."

"Much too far for a girl to go by herself. How could he have done such a thing?"

"Because he knew this was something I wanted to do. He did talk to the train conductor and asked him to keep an eye on me. Does that help ease your mind some?"

"Barely."

Lillian shrugged. "My father loves me and is also trusting of people. He is a simple farmer who has rarely been outside of the town he and I grew up in."

"Did he at least accompany you as far as he could?"

"Yes."

"Good."

"The food should be ready soon. Do you want the beans separate from the bread or on top of it?"

Mr. Williams looked away. "I don't care."

"I don't believe you."

"Why should I care?"

"Because you seem like a picky eater. I'm going to guess that you want them separate. If you don't, you can put the beans on top of the bread yourself."

Mr. Williams grunted.

The food finished a few minutes later, and Lillian found a clean plate to serve them on. She helped him sit up a bit more so he could eat the meal.

"Aren't you going to eat?" he asked.

"No. I ate before I came here and I'll be eating when I get back."

"Back to where?"

"I am staying with Pastor Stuart and his family."

"Oh. Are you a religious fanatic like Pastor Stuart is?"

"I didn't realize he was a fanatic. What do you mean by that?"

"Always wanting to save people from the awful things they do and pushing your beliefs on others."

"Oh. I don't think I'm quite that bad. At least I hope not. I don't want to push my beliefs on people. I just know how God has changed my life and I want the same for them."

"Hm," Mr. Williams grunted as he took a bite of food.

Lillian waited until he finished the food on his plate and then finished slicing the rest of the bread. She brought over the pan of leftover beans and plate of bread and set them on the small table by his bed. "The food is now in reaching distance of you. Whenever you need some, you can dish it up yourself."

"You are leaving now?"

"Yes."

"Good."

"I will try to come back again sometime this week to see how you are doing."

"Don't bother."

"I know you don't care much about yourself and what happens, but I do," Lillian said. "I don't want you to be all alone for too long. I will be back whether you want me to or not."

Mr. Williams grimaced. "I don't have much of a choice, do I?"

"No, you don't. Good day, Mr. Williams."

Lillian left the small cabin and made her way back to the road. Insufferable man. He never did thank her for the food even though he finished it off thoroughly. What had made him such a hardened man? Was it partially due to his wife's death? Or was it the pain that caused him to be so grouchy? Maybe it was a combination of the two.

She should feel good after the errand of mercy she had just finished, so why didn't she?

10

My dear child, There are only a few months left until I see you. I don't know what to think right now. You are moving all the time; sometimes I wonder how much sleep I will get after you are born. If you do not sleep now, will you sleep out here? I certainly hope so. I am so tired right now because you keep me up during the day as well as at night.
But I promised I would not complain. At least if I can feel you moving, I know you are still alive and doing well. You are so precious to both Malachi and me. You will be loved dearly.
Malachi and I finally decided on names. If you are a boy, you will be named after your father, Malachi William Sullivan. If you are a girl, you will be named after my mother, Lillian Carlotta Sullivan. I have always loved my mother's name and am so happy that Malachi agreed with me to let us use that as your name if you are a girl. Although, with all this movement, does that mean you are a boy? Either way, we will both love you dearly, my child.
~ Excerpt from Carlotta Sullivan's memory journal

Curt met her at the livery stable in the same suit he had worn the first day they met. "Are you ready for your first route?"

"I don't know. I hope so, but I'm a bit nervous, too."

"Do you like books?"

"Yes."

"Do you like bringing joy to people?"

"Yes."

"Do you like spending lots of time alone?"

Lillian nodded her head.

"Then you'll do fine. There's plenty of all of those things on these routes. Of course, today, you won't be completely alone since I don't want you getting lost on your first day out. Come, we've a lot to do in a short amount of time. That is, we can talk while we ride."

They mounted their horses. Curt had already slung the saddlebags full of books over her saddle.

As they rode out of town, Curt spoke again. "Pay close attention to where I take you. It shouldn't be too hard once you get used to finding the narrow paths the mountain people take. I have every confidence in you."

"Thank you." Lillian noticed that the route went past Crow Williams' cabin. They made a right-hand turn. "What did you call this route again?"

"The Birch Gap. There are quite a few birches along the route. Some of them so old the white bark isn't white anymore."

Lillian smiled. "I've always loved how pretty the birch trees are. They seem so majestic among all of the brown trunks and green leaves. Don't you think?"

"Do you like poetry, Miss Sullivan?"

"Why do you ask?"

"Because what you said sounded a bit poetic."

"I don't mind a little poetry here and there, but I prefer a straightforward prose."

"Ah, and some big words mixed in a bit, I hear."

Lillian's face grew warm. "I suppose so. Should I refrain from using big words around here?"

"No, no, dear girl. They might think you're uppity, but there's no harm in using some big words now and again. They're likely to ask you to explain yourself, though."

"I should be able to. I loved looking through the dictionary at school during recess. The kids teased me for it, but I did it anyway. I used to memorize big words and their definitions so I could impress the teacher." She sighed. "I had such a crush on that man and he never knew it. I was too shy to tell him and I didn't think it would be right anyway."

Curt glanced at her. "How old were you?"

"Twelve when it started and fourteen when I finally realized he had absolutely no interest in me."

"How did you realize that?"

Lillian cleared her throat. "It's more of a question of where than how. The where was when I saw him kissing a young woman who I later found out was his fiancée. He got married that summer at our church."

Curt's laugh bounced off the hills and trees. "I'm sorry. I don't mean to laugh at you; I just couldn't help it."

"Don't worry about it. I see the humor in it now. Although back then, I needed my father to talk me out of my bad mood."

"How long did that take?"

"Only about two weeks."

"Is that all?"

Lillian caught his eyes and saw the twinkle in them. "Yes, that's all. I'm a romantic. What can I say?"

Curt motioned to the right. "Our first stop is over here."

Lillian followed Curt's lead for the first couple of stops, and then he hung back while she did the book exchange with the people. Most of the time it was the woman of the house who came to the door and took the books. They all seemed a bit reluctant at first, but knew Curt and seemed to accept his recommendation of her.

But one time, a burly, gruff man answered the door. "What do you want?"

Lillian swallowed hard. "I am the new librarian from Willow Hollow. I came to see if you would like a new book to exchange for the one you borrowed from Curt Armstrong a few days ago."

"We haven't finished it yet."

Lillian forced a smile. "Okay. I'll be back in a few days to see if you need a new one yet."

"Thank you."

His polite words nearly knocked her off her feet. She had assumed this man was a younger version of Crow Williams with no manners whatsoever. But he wasn't. "You're welcome." Her smile came easier. "My name is Lillian Sullivan, by the way."

"Martin Gorse."

"A pleasure to meet you, Mr. Gorse."

"Likewise. My boy and I love the books you librarians bring to us. It's the only culture we get up here."

"I'm glad to hear it. What book are you reading right now?"

"Michael, what's the name of the book we're reading?" he shouted behind him.

"*Treasure Island* by Robert Louis Stevenson," a boy's voice answered.

Lillian clasped the book in her hands to her chest. "I loved that book as a child. I may have to read it myself after you finish with it. It has been too long." She looked up at the sky. "Well, I should go. I still have quite a few houses to go to."

"Thank you for stopping, Miss Sullivan."

"You're welcome."

She mounted her horse again and rode off with Curt next to her. "I need to not prejudge people."

"That's always a good thing to learn," Curt said. "Why do you bring that up right now?"

"Because when I saw that man and heard him speak the first time, I thought he was a rude, uncivilized man who would do just about anything without thinking of the consequences. But he's actually a very nice man. Do you know what happened to his wife?"

"She died in childbirth about five years ago."

"Oh dear! The poor man. How old was Michael at the time?"

"He was the child she died giving birth to."

Lillian's heart clenched. Why did childbirth have to be so difficult? Too many good women died much too early, leaving their children motherless. "He hasn't remarried yet?"

"Nope."

"I hope he does," she said softly.

"Why is that? If you don't mind me asking," Curt said.

Lillian didn't answer him for a while. She needed to gather her thoughts first. "I… I grew up motherless. My mother died giving birth to me. Father never remarried. I know it is because there were few eligible women in town, but mail order brides are still possible. I didn't mind so much for myself, but I know how lonely my father got and how much he missed Mother. But a young boy out here in the middle of nowhere, I think he would need a woman's touch to help him not become too shy around women when he grows older."

Curt nodded and was quiet for a short time. "Perhaps when you get to know him better, you can suggest that to him. If you do, you will need to explain why you felt led to say something.

Including sharing that you lost your mother and how that affected you."

"I might just do that," Lillian answered. "Where to next?"

11

*My dear child, as you get to know me, you will come to know that I love
to find the meanings of things. This entry is going to be all about the
meaning of the names we picked out for you.*
*I will start with Lillian because I am really hoping for a girl. The name
Lillian is from the name lily, which is a symbol of purity. Carlotta
means "free man" because it is a feminine version of the name Charles.
Your father's name, Malachi, means "My messenger" or "My
angel" (referring to God). I love this meaning. If you are a boy, I pray
you become a messenger of God and share the gospel with people. Even
if you are a girl, I pray you do so. William means "resolute protector."
Whether you are a boy or a girl, I hope you approve of your name and
can live up to it.*
~ Excerpt from Carlotta Sullivan's memory journal

*L*illian had been on her routes for almost a full week. She
had seen Crow Williams a few times since then on her way
back from her route and had chickened out each time about
telling him about God and His salvation.

Sunday, Lillian sat in church with the Stuart family again
and sang along with the songs. At first, she started to tune out
the sermon as her mind wandered to Crow and how his healing
was going so poorly. Then a phrase the pastor said caught her
attention away from Crow.

"I have been a proud man much of my life. Pride is hard to overcome, but with God all things are possible. But what is it about pride that is difficult to diagnose?" Pastor Stuart stepped away from the pulpit and walked to the side a few steps. "Now you may be thinking, 'Pastor, pride is easy to spot in people. It is also usually easy to spot in yourself.' I don't disagree with you. But there are more subtle forms of pride that are harder to see.

"I thought I had conquered my pride because I had finally started seeing what others needed before I saw to my own needs. But then I did a self-evaluation of myself and realized I had stopped sharing the gospel with people. I had become so wrapped up in seeing the needs of others I had somehow forgotten about their greatest need: salvation. I have come to the conclusion that the greatest form of pride is thinking that someone doesn't need to or want to hear the gospel and be saved. Everyone needs to hear about Christ. Sometimes it takes multiple times before the conviction becomes real enough for them to act. Sometimes it means you have to go out of your comfort zone."

Lillian stopped listening at that point of the sermon. Is this what she had done with Crow? No. It couldn't be. Was she prideful in not wanting to share the gospel with others? She'd had many conversations that lent themselves to focusing on Christ, and she had shied away from them so as to not offend. At least that's what she thought.

As soon as the service finished, Lillian told Patience she needed some time alone and would not be eating lunch with them. Patience looked puzzled but allowed her to go. Lillian returned to the pastor's house, changed into a work dress, wrapped the shawl around herself, grabbed her Bible again, and headed out to the edge of town where she had recently found a beautiful little spot with low-hanging trees she could climb into without being immodest. Once there, she found her favorite tree and pulled herself up into it.

She set the Bible in her lap and closed her eyes. The air was cool, but not overly cold. Unlike in Montana where she would be freezing to death by now. Lillian took a deep breath and prayed silently, *Lord, I need to know what I have been doing wrong. Have I been prideful in not sharing Your gospel to Crow and the others on my route? I know my main reason for wanting to come out here was to share the gospel and I have yet to do that. Is that a sin? I didn't think so until Pastor preached his sermon. Now I'm not so sure. What must I do? Help me, Lord.*

Lillian opened her Bible to her favorite book in the Bible, Philippians, and started reading. As she started chapter two, a verse popped out at her. "Do nothing from selfishness or empty conceit, but with humility of mind regard one another as more important than yourselves…" She stopped and thought back on the last few weeks here in Willow Hollow. She had done more for herself than others here. She needed to refocus her thought process on others and not herself. But how?

She kept reading in Philippians chapter two.

…do not merely look out for your own personal interests, but also for the interests of others. Have this attitude in yourselves which was also in Christ Jesus, who, although He existed in the form of God, did not regard equality with God a thing to be grasped, but emptied Himself, taking the form of a bond-servant, and being made in the likeness of men. Being found in appearance as a man, He humbled

Himself by becoming obedient to the point of death,
even death on a cross.

Of course. It was that simple. Just imitate Christ. She should be doing that anyway, but it was no easy task. She needed to write some thoughts down. She pulled a piece of paper out of the front of her Bible and the pencil from her dress pocket and started writing a list.

~ Read Bible daily
~ Pray at least half an hour daily
~ Reflect on ways to serve others rather than self
~ Find at least one person every day to talk to about God and actually do it
~ Don't chicken out
~ Pray before entering each home

She tapped the end of the pencil on her Bible and stared at the list. This seemed like a good start at least. She could always add to the list as she thought of other things. For now she would keep it simple and to the point. Because she needed that. Anything more would be too overwhelming and cause her to rebel against what she set for herself.

For now, she should get back to the Stuarts' home and let them know she was all right. Then she would start implementing her list.

12

My dear child, The doctor came today to check on me. I am getting ever closer to that wonderful day when I get to meet you. It is still a couple months away, but it is becoming more real to me. You move a lot inside of me. I have a feeling you are going to be an active little one who will keep me very busy trying to keep you out of things. But I look forward to that.
~ Excerpt from Carlotta Sullivan's memory journal

*M*onday. The first day since her resolve to share the gospel with at least one person. She should feel incredibly nervous but somehow wasn't. Maybe it was her prayer or the reading of her Bible that morning. She didn't know and it didn't matter. What mattered was that she was ready to do whatever she needed to do that day.

Lillian saddled her horse and loaded some books into the saddlebags at the library. Curt bade her farewell and then she was on her own. She was still learning the names of some of the people on her route, but otherwise, she had the route down perfectly. Her favorite people to visit were those with children. The children who were allowed to be near her always seemed so excited to receive new books to read. They reminded her of herself when she was their age. She had loved reading. It was a way of escape and a way to find out what a family was like who had both a mother and father.

Mrs. Peterson had been a help whenever she needed a woman to talk to, but she had been no substitute for a mother. Only by reading did she learn what she was missing by not having a mother to teach her how to cook and clean, and to care for her.

Lillian shook her head. Of all the things to be thinking about today, why this? She didn't need to arrive at the first home all sad and depressed. She needed to be upbeat and happy. *Think happy thoughts*, she said to herself. Thoughts about her father and how much he loved her and took care of her even on the most difficult of days. A smile crept onto her face as she remembered a time when she had been sick and her father had stayed by her bedside all day and fell asleep at the foot of her bed that night. Lillian had woken up in the middle of the night needing some water, but decided to not bother her father and let him sleep instead.

Before she could finish the memory, the first home came into view. She talked to the man and his son for a bit, but there were no openings to share the gospel without an awkward transition, so she moved on to the next place. And the next and the next. Surely somewhere on this route she would find someone to talk to without forcing the issue.

Finally, towards the end of her route, Opal asked her a question. "You always seem to be smiling every time you come here. Why is that?"

Lillian smiled reflexively. "It probably has at least a little to do with the fact that I get to talk about books all day long. But it probably also has to do with my faith in God."

The woman, Opal, blinked slowly. "God? You mean the one the preacher in town is always railing about?"

Lillian stifled a laugh. "I wouldn't personally call it railing, but yes."

"If it's not railin', what is it? He talks all about how God wants us to go to hell and how awful we are, especially if we're superstitious or drink the moonshine the Higginses make."

Lillian shuffled a little. She had her work cut out for her here. "Well, first of all, I'm sorry you understood him that way. That isn't what he meant at all. Do you mind if I try to explain a little more?"

Opal beckoned for her to come in the house. Lillian followed her into the dark home. The house needed a few windows, but it was livable. She sat on one of the wooden chairs around the table and waited until Opal poured them both a cup of tea. "I would offer you coffee, but I am running low."

Lillian shook her head. "I don't drink much coffee anyway. I much prefer tea."

"Good. Now the first thing I would like to know is what did I misunderstand about God wanting us to go to hell?"

Lillian took in a deep breath. "The Bible says that 'God so loved the world that He gave His only begotten Son that whosoever believeth in Him shall not perish, but have eternal life.' God loves everyone in the whole world and wants all of us to go to heaven—to have eternal life—rather than perish, or go to hell. If Pastor Stuart mentioned hell, it was to show what God does to those who refuse His free gift of salvation."

"It's free to get to heaven? You don't have to do nothin'?"

Lillian smiled. "No, you don't. All you have to do is believe that Jesus died on the cross for your sins, rose from the dead after three days, and is now living with His Father in heaven waiting to bring you up to live with Him forever."

"Why don't more people do it then?"

"I'm not sure. Sometimes I think they just want to keep living their own way and not in obedience to Christ."

Opal huffed. "That just sounds plain crazy to me. I can't imagine being that stubborn-headed." Her mouth made an O. "But then again, I can think of a few people in these here hills that would be that stubborn. I want to know more about that accepting of God's gift later, but first tell me about why Pastor said we're all awful people."

Lillian tried to hold back a smile but failed. "Do you remember these verses? 'For all have sinned and fall short of the glory of God.' And 'For the wages of sin is death.'"

Opal bit her lip. "They sound familiar."

"Pastor probably quoted them or read them from his Bible. The first one means that everyone in the whole world has sinned and there is no way we can work our way to heaven by doing good works to outweigh our bad. The second verse means that we deserve death for our sins. But Jesus came and lived a perfect life, then sacrificed Himself on the cross willingly to pay for *our* sins so we can go live with Him in heaven someday."

Opal leaned forward. "He did that for me?"

Lillian nodded. "He did."

"How do I accept the free gift?"

Lillian silently thanked God for His working. "All you have to do is pray to God. Just talk to Him like you would to me. Tell Him how you know you are a sinner and believe Jesus died on the cross for those sins and that you want to be His child. John 1:12 says, 'But as many as received Him, to them gave He power to become the sons of God, even to them that believe on His name.'"

"Is there any special way to pray to God?"

"No. I usually either sit or kneel and then fold my hands, but you can do it however you would like. I have also prayed while riding my horse or doing the dishes, so folding the hands is optional as well."

Opal smiled. "Can you stay here while I do it?"

"Of course."

Opal took a deep breath and folded her hands. "Hi, God. It's me, Opal. Thanks for sending Lillian here to talk to me. I needed this today and it really helped explain some things I didn't understand. From those verses, I know that I'm a sinner. I've done lots wrong, but I don't want to anymore. I want the free gift that You offer. I believe Jesus died for me and then rose again. I want to be Your child and come live with You in heaven someday. Thank you, God."

"Amen," Lillian said.

Opal looked over at her. "Was I supposed to say that?"

"No, I just felt like saying it."

Opal rose and pulled Lillian up into a tight hug. "Thank you, Lillian. I feel so different. What can I do to keep this feeling and to learn more about God?"

"Do you have a Bible?"

"Yes. We have a family Bible."

"Read it. I personally love the book of Saint John, but you can start wherever you would like."

"I always start books at the beginning."

"You can do that if you would like. Just know that not all the books of the Bible are like the first five books."

Opal raised her eyebrows. "What do you mean?"

"Well, I personally find that most of Exodus, Numbers, Leviticus, and Deuteronomy is rather dry."

"Now you have me even more curious. I'll read them for myself and find out."

Lillian glanced outside. "It's getting late and I still have a couple of stops. It was so nice to talk to you today."

Opal gave her another hug. "Yes, it was. Thank you for being brave enough to talk like that."

"You're welcome."

13

My dearest child, You are starting to keep your mother awake already and you aren't even out of my womb yet. Does this mean you will not sleep well at night as a baby? I certainly hope not. As much as I love you, I need a little sleep at night. Maybe if I sing a lullaby to you at night before I go to bed. I will have to try that tonight.
~ Excerpt from Carlotta Sullivan's memory journal

*L*illian returned to the Stuarts' home with a giddy feeling all over her. She wanted to tell someone what had happened but didn't know how. Was it boasting to say something about it? That depended on how she shared it. If she said it pridefully, it would be boasting. However, if she were to simply inform them politely, she would not be boasting. If it was easy enough to interject into the conversation, she would do it. If not, she would wait or not say anything at all.

She rode into the livery yard and Jed came out to meet her.

"Productive day on the trail?"

"Always. The mountain people are really embracing reading with a passion."

Jed smirked. "I love hearing you talk. It's so different from the others 'round here."

"How?"

He shrugged. "It seems a bit more poetic. You just said 'embracing reading with a passion' when we would've said something like 'starting to love reading.'"

"Do I do that a lot?"

Jed nodded.

"I didn't realize that."

"You wouldn't have. It's natural to you, but not to us, so we notice it more readily." Jed took the reins to her horse as she dismounted. "I'll take care of her for you. You go on to the house. Ma's almost got supper ready."

"Thank you, Jed. You are a very kind young man."

Jed's face reddened. "You're welcome."

The dinner was delicious as always, but the conversation never strayed to a way for Lillian to share her news, so she decided that was God's way of saying, "Be quiet about it for now, child." When she went to bed, she said an extra special thanks to God for working through her. And prayed that she would have the courage to plant a few seeds at the very least in Crow's life when she visited him next.

Three days after sharing with Opal, Lillian made her way on foot to Crow Williams' cabin. She tapped on the door lightly.

"You're lucky I ain't deaf, girl. Come to talk my ear off?"

Lillian smiled as she pushed the door open. "Good morning, Mr. Williams. Last I checked, you still had two ears."

"Crow."

"Crow. And as you know, I am always willing to hear you talk, but you never want to."

"That's because I don't like people."

"And I don't believe you."

Crow huffed. "Why not?"

"Because each visit I make, you are less grumpy."

Crow scowled. Or rather, attempted to, but Lillian could tell he was secretly pleased by her observation. "Well, what'dya want to talk about this week?"

"Have you ever been to church?"

Crow visibly tensed. "A couple of times."

"What were your opinions of it?"

"I didn't like it. No one there liked me. They all judged me."

Lillian sighed. "I'm sorry to hear that. I wish things had been different for you there. But it shouldn't be that way. People can be cruel. I used to judge people for what they wore and how they looked all the time. Then I changed. I knew I needed to stop, and I slowly but surely changed. I started being kind to people and seeing them the way God would see them rather than the way people see them. And you know what? It changed more than just the way I saw people. It also changed the way I treated them, the way I acted around them, and the way I thought.

"But not everybody can do that. Not everyone wants to change or has the ability to. Most people don't even know they need to change. I don't know why that is and I wish it could be different."

Crow kept his eyes on her face the whole time she spoke, his eyes seeming to soften as she finished. "You sure talk well, Lillian. The first thing I noticed 'bout you 'sides how wet you were is that you looked at me all judgmental. I didn't want to admit it. What is it about you that is so different?"

"I don't know for sure besides that God's done a major work in me."

"What about the previous times we talked? You've always been a sweet girl, but there's something different today."

Lillian ducked her head. "I have always been shy. I didn't mind it though. It kept me out of awkward conversations with people. I thought it was okay to be shy until recently. Pastor Stuart preached a sermon about pride, and I realized I had been using my shyness as a shield so I wouldn't have to share the best thing of my life with people. I knew I needed to change that and have done so since the sermon last week. It will be a process, I'm sure. I still don't use some opportunities I get, but I try when I can."

"Like today."

Lillian smiled. "Yes."

"What is this best thing you mentioned?"

Lillian sat on the edge of his bed with a Bible open and a smile permanently fixed to her face as she shared the gospel with the injured and dying old man. He did not become a Christian that day as Lillian had hoped, but he promised to think about what she said, and she prayed that sometime before his death, Crow would see his need for Christ and take it.

She left Crow's house happy despite not receiving an immediate decision from Crow. Today had been the first day he had not insulted her or tried to bring her down in some way.

Two days later, she rode past Crow's house on her way home and decided to make a quick stop before finishing her journey to town. She stepped inside. Crow appeared gaunt and withered in the bed. Lillian tried not to show her feelings as she approached his bed.

"I heard you ride in," Crow said, his voice raspy.

"I didn't exactly keep it a secret," Lillian answered with a forced laugh.

"I did it."

Lillian blinked. "Did what?"

"Prayed like you said to. Didn't know this kind of peace was possible. Thank you for sharing Christ with me so I could feel it before I die."

Tears sprang to Lillian's eyes and she threw her arms gently around him. "God be praised. I am so happy for you. I don't think I could have borne it if you died without knowing Christ."

"I have a favor to ask of you."

Lillian wiped the tears off her cheeks and nodded. "Anything."

"I want you to talk to the pastor after I die. I want him to do the funeral, but I also want you to read something from me. Do you have something to write with and on?"

Lillian stood and hurried outside to her saddlebags, where she pulled out a notepad and pencil, then rushed back inside. "I rarely go somewhere without these."

Crow smiled. The first genuine smile she had ever seen on him. "I'm ready."

Lillian had a hard time writing what she wrote as tears flooded her eyes again and again, but she persevered through his statement. "I can't guarantee I won't cry while I read this," she said, "but I will read this for you."

"Thank you. You have been like the daughter or granddaughter I never had. I hate to burden you with such a task, but I am grateful we had a chance to meet and get to know each other."

Lillian's lips quivered. "I am grateful for that as well. I never knew either of my grandfathers, so I will always consider you the adopted grandfather I got to know for a few weeks."

"It's getting too dark. Go home now. I don't want you to be hurt."

Lillian patted his cheek affectionately. "Yes, sir."

Crow captured her hand before she could remove it from his cheek. "God bless you, dear Lillian."

"Thank you."

14

The lullaby singing hasn't helped yet, but I am not going to give up on it.
If it still continues to be so bad, I'll have to try sleeping on my right side
instead of my left side. Perhaps that will work instead.
~ Excerpt from Carlotta Sullivan's memory journal

*M*arch arrived with sunshine and warm days. Lillian marveled at how different the weather here could be from Montana. She loved the weather here, especially as she traveled the countryside with the books. Doing this in Montana would have been dangerous. But here in Kentucky, the most danger she could find was the wild animals and even those seemed to avoid her as much as she avoided them.

Every few days after sharing the gospel with Crow, Lillian stopped at his cabin to visit him. She had tried to read the Bible to him every time she went and he devoured every word.

The first Tuesday of March, she rode up to his cabin, loosely tied her horse to the post outside, and knocked on the door before entering.

Not a peep from Crow. Even with his newfound faith and kindness, Crow still said something when she entered his house; it was just usually kinder than it had been in the past.

"Mr. Williams?" She approached his bed with caution. His eyes were closed and he lay perfectly still. Was he only asleep? Or was there something else?

She tentatively reached out her hand and touched his shoulder. Through the shirt she could tell he was cold. Her hand jerked back and a sob escaped her from somewhere deep inside.

He couldn't be gone. He was alive just days ago. She rocked back onto the soles of her feet, tears streaming down her face. How had he died so fast? Sure, he had been hurt and she knew he would die soon, but this seemed so sudden. Had he needed help and she hadn't been there?

Why, oh why hadn't she stopped in more often? And where had the doctor been?

Lillian turned around and darted outside. Once out of the house she looked around at the trees. Where could she go? What did she need to do? She couldn't let him stay here. She needed to get him somewhere. There was an undertaker just down the street from the church. She should get him there. She wished he had family to tell but knew he didn't know, hadn't known, where they were.

All of these thoughts passed through Lillian's mind, but she couldn't move. Her body refused to work for her. She had too much work to do to stand here endlessly.

When her sobs subsided, Lillian went into action. She needed to get him to the undertaker quickly and start working with the pastor on funeral arrangements. But she couldn't get him to the undertaker by herself.

She rushed out to her horse, jumped up onto her, and rode like mad to town. At the livery stable, she barely let the horse stop before jumping off of her. "Jed! I need your help and a cart."

Jed peeked his head out of the stable door. "What's going on?"

She swallowed past the lump in her throat. "Mr. Williams died. I need to get him...his body to the undertaker."

Jed stared at her for a few seconds before retreating back to the stable. A minute later, he came out leading a horse who pulled a cart. "Lead the way."

Lillian mounted her horse again and led him to Crow's cabin. Together, Jed and Lillian managed to get Crow's body into the cart. Lillian rummaged around his house for a suit or some kind of newer clothes the undertaker could bury him in, but found nothing.

"What are you doing?" Jed asked.

"I wanted to find some nice clothes to bury Crow in."

Jed shook his head. "Mr. Williams didn't have any and I don't think anyone would recognize him in them. He'd rather be in his flannel shirt, jeans, and coonskin hat."

Lillian picked up the hat and let out a long breath. "You're right. Let's go."

As they went to town, Lillian followed the cart to make sure Crow's body didn't bounce out. They dropped him off and then Lillian went to the church to talk to Pastor Stuart.

"Pastor?"

"Lillian. Are you all right?"

Lillian nodded, then shook her head. "Mr. Williams died."

Pastor Stuart took her arm and led her to one of the pews. "I'm sorry to hear that. I know you were getting close to him."

Lillian nodded again. "I didn't know you could get so close to someone in less than a month. But I also know that I'll see him again some day in heaven, and that is comforting. But I actually came to talk about his funeral arrangements."

"Of course. I'll do whatever I can. Do you know what he wanted?"

"He wanted you to do the funeral service for him. He asked me to read something for him as well. I have it in my room at your house. I can get it for you if you want to see it ahead of time."

"No, that's fine. I don't need to see everything. Do you know if he had any preference for anything for the service?"

"No. I don't think he had ever been to a funeral at a church and only recently read the Bible." Lillian stopped as tears welled up in her eyes again.

"I'll do my generic funeral then. Do you need someone to go get him to the undertaker?"

"No. I had Jed help me."

Pastor Stuart nodded with the slightest of smiles. "Very well. I will talk to the undertaker and most likely plan on doing the funeral in the afternoon the day after tomorrow. Let me know if you need anything else."

"Thank you."

Lillian left the church and wandered around the town aimlessly until it got too dark to see. Then she returned to the Stuart house and picked at her supper while the family ate and talked. After the meal, Abigail came over to her and gave her a hug. Nothing else. No words, just a hug. But it was just what Lillian needed and didn't know she did.

Two days later, a few people from town gathered to lay Crow Williams to rest behind the church. Lillian tuned out what Pastor Stuart said until he said that she had something to read.

She took a deep breath and unfolded the piece of paper in her hand. "About a week ago, Mr. Williams asked me to write this up and read it to you when we had the funeral." She looked over the few faces in the crowd. There were so few of them. The doctor, the Stuart family, a couple older men she didn't recognize. "I told him I would try, but I couldn't guarantee I wouldn't cry."

She looked down at the paper and started reading.

I know very few people in Willow Hollow liked me. I was a crotchety old man who didn't care about anyone in my life. At least that's what I made it seem like. I grew up in this town, but lived apart from the people in it 'cuz that's what everyone did. We weren't as friendly as you are now. I married a wonderful woman the day I turned twenty-one. She was eighteen. I loved her more than I'd ever loved another human being. We had twenty-five happy years together. We had two boys who we tried to raise right.

When she died suddenly for no apparent reason, I became even more mean and sullen. Then a month ago, I met this young lady. I'm not as poetic as she is, but we met under some not-so-nice circumstances and I got badly injured. The doctor didn't give me much hope of living and I could feel it in my bones that he was right. I wouldn't survive these injuries. The doc brought me to my home to die at my request. I expected I would be there by myself the whole time with only the rare visit from the doc. But Lillian surprised me with her first visit.

I figured she visited me out of guilt and at first I think that was the case. As time went on, we got to be friends. Before asking her to write this up for me, I told her that I consider her the daughter or granddaughter I never had. In fact, if this can count for a will, I give all my belongings and money—such as it is—to Lillian.

Lillian choked on her tears as she read that part, and she took a minute to recover her composure.

Most of all, I wanted everybody to know that Lillian was more than just a granddaughter to me. She also told me about Jesus Christ and how He died for all of us. I am a Christian now and the only reason I am one is because of her. Of course, God is the main reason, but He used Lillian. I wish there was a way to make up for all the meanness and hatred I had for everyone, but I know there isn't. God forgave me for my sins and now I ask that you forgive me as well. Since asking God to save me, I have been praying for everyone I know by name. Know that I love you all and hope to see you in heaven someday.

Crow Williams

Lillian took a step backward and Pastor Stuart finished the service. Lillian felt a hand on her shoulder and an arm around her waist and looked around to see Patience Stuart and Abigail flanking her. Tears streamed down her face and she put the note from Crow back into her skirt pocket. Her friend was gone, but he was in a better place now.

15

My dearest child, If the doctor is correct, you will be here in about four weeks. Thankfully, you have settled down some at night, but now whenever I get up, I feel absolutely huge and so clumsy I am afraid I will fall. But I always make it there safely.
~ Excerpt from Carlotta Sullivan's memory journal

*L*illian entered the small room. Curt already sat at the table in the chair nearest the door. Lillian moved to his right and sat next to him. One of the other librarians, Edna, had already arrived and sat at Curt's left with a lot of space between her and Curt.

"You're here early," Curt stated.

Lillian nodded. "I didn't have anything else to do this morning."

Curt put a hand on her arm. "How are you doing?"

Lillian shrugged. "I've been better, but I am coping." She glanced at the woman across from her. She had a severe spinsterish look about her, but Lillian thought she might be kinder than she looked. Lena entered quietly a minute later and sat next to Lillian, opening a book immediately.

Curt kept checking his watch. Lillian wanted to break into the silence somehow, but didn't know what to say. She didn't really know the woman across from her yet, and Lena always rebuffed her attempts at conversation.

Edna made a last scratch in her notebook and closed it with a not-so-quiet slap. She gave Curt a pointed look. "How long are we going to wait for?"

Curt gave a sheepish shrug. "I'm sure she'll be along any moment."

"Isn't she staying here at the Building?" Edna asked.

Curt scratched behind his ear. "She'll…be along in just a minute, I'm sure."

Lena looked up from her book and Lillian cocked her head. Why hadn't he answered her question directly? Where was this new librarian truly staying?

Curt glanced at all of them. "She's a delightful gal, and I'm sure you'll be as impressed as I am with her."

"If she ever arrives," Edna muttered, sitting back and folding her arms across her chest.

Curt fidgeted with the hem of his dark-blue coat. "I'm… sure she'll be along any moment."

A blond-haired woman burst into the room with a great smile as if being late didn't bother anyone else in the room. Her gaze swept the room quickly. "Good morning, everyone!" Her sky-blue dress with lace trimming was worn, but not as threadbare as many of the women in town.

Lillian stared at her briefly and tried to think of something to say, but Edna beat her to it.

"Good grief," Edna muttered. "It's Shirley Temple."

Lillian wasn't sure who that was exactly, but knew the girl referenced was an actress in one of the moving pictures she had never seen.

Curt stepped toward Ivory and laid a hand on her shoulder. "I-I'd like you to meet our new librarian."

Lillian watched Ivory with curiosity.

The blond librarian's smile seemed to falter ever so slightly, but she rattled out words anyway. "I'm so happy to finally meet everyone. I've been here for near a week now and"—she giggled—"other than my five-year-old friend, Gerrit... oh, and Mr. Armstrong, of course... I haven't met hardly a soul."

Everyone kept watching her with curious eyes. Lillian opened her mouth to say something, but didn't.

Curt tried again. "Ladies, this here is Miss Ivory Bledsoe. She's come to us from around Nashville."

Edna raised her brow and reopened her notebook, obviously too busy to pay much more attention to Ivory's introduction.

Curt swallowed, then nodded, gripping Ivory's shoulder as if it brought him comfort instead of her. "Can you tell us why you're here, that is, why you decided to come to Willow Hollow?"

Ivory nodded and slid a step away from Curt's touch. "To share books." She beamed wider. "I heard what y'all were doing here, what President Roosevelt was doing here, and I just had to help." She pressed both hands to her heart and blinked away the wetness in her eyes. "I read about how lonely the people in the mountains are and how few books they had to read, and... no one should live without a friend and a good book." She gave a slight shrug. "So here I am." She continued to grin through the silence, batting away the emotion in her eyes. Pulling in a strong breath, she tried again, "I must say, your town doesn't begin to compare with the city. It's beautiful here. I knew it would be. I heard it would be. But... boy, golly! These mountains sure do take my breath away!"

Lena's eyes lifted to meet Ivory's but skittered away after brushing contact.

Lillian finally spoke softly. "I'm new here myself and I agree, it's lovely. It reminds me a lot of my home, but warmer."

Edna looked up from her notes and scanned Ivory from head to toe. "Are you sending her out on the trail?" she asked Curt.

Curt moved closer and rested his hand on Ivory's shoulder again. "She'll stay here with me; that is, she has a place working in the office with me."

Ivory's smile slipped again. "I brought hundreds of new books with me."

Lena's face brightened and she looked to the wall where the boxes sat. Lillian joined her excitement. New books were just the distraction she needed.

"I'm going to help get the library organized and be here to help recommend books to your patrons from the new selection."

Curt pointed to his right where Lillian sat at the rectangle table. "This is Miss Lillian Sullivan. Like she mentioned, she's new here, too."

Lillian smiled at her, and Ivory circled Curt and the table to lean in for a hug, which Lillian returned with slight hesitation. "Then we should have loads in common! Where are you from?"

"Montana," she stated.

Ivory's eyes lit up. "Golly! And I thought I was far from home!"

Next Curt turned to Lena.

Ivory leaned in for a hug before Curt could even say her name.

"And this is Miss Lena Davis. She sure loves to read." Curt warmly chuckled. "You'll find her in the library before it opens." He sent her a brotherly smile, but Lena dropped her eyes to the cover of her book.

Ivory's grin somehow brightened even more. "So we're destined to be best friends, you and I!"

Lena darted a glance at Ivory that Lillian couldn't quite decipher.

Curt pointed to Edna, who sat directly to his left. "This here is Miss Edna O'Connell. She's a local girl."

"Woman," Edna stated.

"Huh? What's that?" Curt frowned in puzzlement.

"I'm an adult. I'm a local woman—well, by extraction, at least."

Curt didn't seem to understand her point, but it didn't matter because Ivory charged around the table. "I'm pleased as punch to meet you."

"So I see." Edna tapped the tip of her pencil against her notebook page and eyed Ivory dispassionately.

Ivory moved like she was about to hug her, but Edna turned her shoulder and faced Curt as if she didn't see her. Ivory gave up and settled in the seat beside Edna. Edna moved her chair a smidgen away from Ivory.

"So what of the meeting?" Edna asked.

Curt settled into his chair. "The big news is, we're expanding. With the new books Ivory, that is, Miss Bledsoe, has brought us"—he paused slightly to smile at her—"we have enough to open a new route."

Lillian joined the ladies in expressions of satisfaction. Edna didn't respond, other than to listen attentively.

"I have it here on the map." Curt shuffled through his papers and unfolded his map of the region. "We're going to take on new territory in Possum Valley, and I want you to see to them, Edna."

Edna sat up straighter and studied the area marked out in pencil lines. "Will I need to give up my usual Lazy Bear route?"

"No." Curt paused. "Of course, your salary will be increased."

The frown lines eased on her face. She appeared relieved, almost happy. "By how much?" she asked bluntly.

"Uh, let me see if I have the figure here. Here it is. By fifty percent. So that would be an additional fourteen dollars per month. Would... would that be okay?"

"Yes, that's satisfactory." Edna sat back in her chair.

"But that's not all. They're opening a new library in Steven's Gap. Until they have proper staffing, I'm going to be splitting my time there as well. And Ivory will be a large help to me here in my absence."

Just then a rush of commotion shot through the door. Gerrit Callon rushed in, heading straight for Ivory. He was grubby and had green eyes and more blondish than strawberry-blond hair.

"Miss Ivory, Miss Ivory, I'm ready for my story!" Only after he reached her side did he take in the people around him. He took his arms off Ivory and scrambled up in the chair beside her. "Oh, do I get to be one of 'em book fellas again, too?"

Curt started to say no, but Ivory was already saying that he could as long as he was super quiet. Lillian smiled at the energy of the little boy. Curt, Ivory, and Gerrit seemed to have a special relationship with each other already.

Gerrit leaned forward and grinned proudly at Edna. "See there, Edna? I'm a book man like you is!"

Edna gave him a slight smile and a barely perceptible nod of her head.

Ivory noticed Edna's response and asked, "Is Edna your friend, too?"

Gerrit gave a slight nod. "She's my cousin."

Ivory looked to both, then to Lillian. "Is Lillian your cousin, too?"

"I don't reckon." He paused to eye Lillian. "Are you my cousin?"

Lillian chuckled softly. "No, but I'm staying with the Stuarts, and I believe Mrs. Stuart might be your cousin."

"How delightful!" Ivory exclaimed.

Edna's mouth lifted in a small smile.

Curt cleared his throat. "Now that that's settled, let's continue, shall we?"

More business was discussed, but none of it really related to Lillian except the new books, so she didn't say much. She would love another route but knew there were people who needed the routes more than she, so she would let them have their pick first. After the meeting ended, Lillian tried to avoid Ivory but was unable to escape as quickly as Edna had.

"Lillian," Ivory squealed, bounding toward her. "When can we get together? I've had a time trying to fit in here and wondered if you'd have any advice for me?"

Lillian smiled. "I don't know how much I can help you. I came from a small town to a small town. You came from a rather large town."

Her face fell but just as quickly she brightened back into a smile. "Can we talk anyway? I've been just dying to get to know the people here." She cast a look from side to side and dropped her voice. "Most of the people I've met haven't been near as friendly toward me."

"Are you available now? I don't have a route short enough to do today anyway."

"Hotdog! I have all the time in the world." She froze. "Oh, hang on." Ivory turned and called out to Curt. "Mr. Armstrong?

109

Can you spare me this morning?" Setting her hand on Lillian's arm, she continued, "I've found a friend to—"

His smile split his face. "Go right ahead, Miss Bledsoe," he interrupted.

Ivory turned back to Lillian, her face beaming with excitement.

16

My dear child, I have a feeling you are coming earlier than the doctor expected. I might be wrong, but I have had these pains before with my other birth. If they intensify much more, I will be sending your father to get the doctor. For now, I'll just lie here writing to you while he sleeps. Why is it that all of my children have seemed to want to be born at night?
~ Excerpt from Carlotta Sullivan's memory journal

The day after the meeting, Lillian went about her routes almost mindlessly. She talked to people and tried to be as cheerful and friendly as before, but people noticed. Especially Opal. When Opal asked if she was okay, Lillian was embarrassed when she broke out sobbing.

Sweet Opal put her arms around Lillian and let her sob into her shoulder until she had no more tears left. "What happened?"

"Crow Williams died."

"The old man who you have been talking to?"

Lillian nodded.

"Oh, Lillian. I am so sorry to hear that."

"I knew it would happen soon, but somehow I thought it would take longer. And I shouldn't even be that sad. He was a Christian, so he is in a better place, but I miss him."

"As you should. I know you didn't know him long, but you probably got to know him better than anyone else in this area. And you have a very caring personality. It is normal for you to miss him and want to cry about it once in a while."

"Even though I know I will see him again someday?"

"Yes."

Lillian let herself out of Opal's arms. "Thank you."

Opal smiled. "You're welcome. Now tell me, did you share the gospel with anyone today?"

"Not yet, but I promise to talk more to the next patron."

"I'm glad you got your crying out here, then. And I won't keep you. Just give me my book and be on your way."

Lillian smiled despite her tears. "Yes, ma'am."

Almost every day on the trail, Lillian tried to mention God to at least one person, sometimes talking in depth about Him and sometimes just keeping it casual. Not everyone was receptive, but others were.

One day about two weeks after Crow's funeral, Jed asked if he could come along for her shorter day of routes.

"Why?"

He shrugged. "I'm curious what all you do. Besides, I think there's a bad storm coming through and I don't want you stuck in it, or if you do get stuck in it, I don't want you stuck alone."

Lillian gave him a playful punch in the shoulder. "I always wished I had a brother. After meeting you, I really wish it."

"I can be your adopted brother," Jed said.

Lillian grinned. "I'd like that. Come on, brother Jed. Let's go deliver books to people."

They were almost finished with the route when Jed slowed his horse down.

"What is it?" Lillian asked.

"Do you smell that?"

Lillian sniffed. "Nothing different than I usually smell out here."

"I smell rain. We should find shelter before it really starts."

Lillian raised an eyebrow but decided to trust him.

Jed led the way down a narrow path to a small cabin surrounded by a small clearing. There was a buggy tied to the post. Lillian glanced at Jed but didn't say anything. Who could be here besides the person who lived in the cabin?

Jed dismounted and knocked on the door. The doctor opened it.

"What do you want?" the doctor asked.

"There's a bad storm coming. Can we take shelter with you and the owner of the cabin?"

The doctor looked behind him and spotted Lillian. "Fine. Come on in."

Jed helped Lillian off her horse. "I'll take care of the horses. You go inside."

Lillian nodded. With a calming breath, she made her way into the house past the imposing doctor. "Who are you attending to here?"

The doctor gestured toward a dark corner where an older woman lay sleeping in a bed.

"Oh," Lillian whispered. "What is she sick of?"

The doctor sat on one of the chairs. "Nothing anymore."

Lillian glanced between him and the old woman. "She's—"

The doctor nodded.

Lillian looked away, her breath coming in short, raspy gasps. This couldn't be happening again. She couldn't be in a small cabin with a dead body again. *Why, God, why? Why couldn't the rain hold off a little longer?* She turned away from the bed and sat at the table so she wouldn't have to look at it.

"All the horses are in the barn. I put your buggy in there too so you won't have to drive on a wet seat on the way home, Doctor."

"Thank you, Jed," the doctor said.

"What shall we talk about while we are stuck here?" Jed asked.

"Nothing," Dr. Casey stated.

"We can't just sit here and stare at each other. Whose house is this?"

"It was old woman McFeely's," Dr. Casey answered. "Now I suppose it belongs to her children, but they won't be coming back to claim it."

"Why not?" Lillian questioned.

Jed sat at the table with them. "I know that one. They left town a long time ago. As soon as they all became adults. Mrs. McFeely wrote to them when she could, but never got answers. None of them ever came back to Willow Hollow even to visit their mother."

Lillian's chest clenched. "How sad. How could anyone do that to their own mother?"

Jed shook his head. "I don't know. I never knew her kids; I just heard the story of them never coming back."

"Let's talk about something else," Lillian said with a shudder.

"Like what?" Jed asked.

Lillian looked from Jed to the doctor and back again. "Dr. Casey, why don't you ever come to church?"

Dr. Casey tensed. "I promised my mother I would never go to church, and I will not break that promise."

Lillian gasped. "Why would you promise such a thing?"

"My mother hated the church and everything it represented. I never saw any reason to not hate it myself, so I made the promise before she died and have never gone."

"Have you ever been told what the Bible and church is all about?" Jed asked.

"No. And I don't care to."

"But how do you know you don't care to if you don't even know what is going to be said?" Jed narrowed his eyes. "Are you afraid you might actually want to change your mind?"

Dr. Casey glared at him. "No. It seems you are determined to tell me something, so go ahead. I'll listen, but that is the only thing I can promise."

Lillian's gloom started to lift slightly at his words. Maybe this was why God hadn't had the rain hold off longer. Jed and Lillian took turns talking about the gospel and the Bible and what church really was like and how they had all changed their lives. The doctor listened, but that's all he did. He didn't answer any of their questions or ask any.

Lillian tried to decipher the look on his face, but it was too blank. Were they wasting their time talking to him? No, even if he wasn't paying super close attention, he had to hear at least parts of what they said.

They finally ran out of things to say and stopped. After a silence of just over a minute, Lillian asked, "Do you have anything to say?"

"No. I haven't changed my mind if that is what you are asking."

Lillian's heart sank. "Why not?"

"I don't know. I guess I don't need religion."

Lillian heard Jed saying something, but tuned out. What had they done wrong? Why hadn't he at least had a little bit of a change of heart? Even her most reluctant patrons she had talked to had thanked her for telling them and promised to think about what she had said. Why this? Why now? She closed her eyes and tried to keep the sinking feeling from going any lower than her chest.

The rain continued for hours. Darkness filled the cabin. Lillian made them some food out of Mrs. McFeely's supplies and made sure the fire kept going. She needed to keep busy, so she also cleaned up the cabin as much as she could without going too close to the bed.

Jed and the doctor chatted and played checkers together while Lillian worked. She wanted the rain to be finished. She looked out the window and stared at the steady streams of water. It was coming down harder than she had seen. If it had been colder, this would have been blizzard weather with the wind and the heavy precipitation. But instead it was rain that looked to be washing away the grass. Unless the shadows were playing tricks on her eyes, which was very possible. Lillian could think of nothing good coming from this rain.

17

I was right. The doctor is here now, so this will be brief. I just want you
to know that I love you. No matter what. You are my precious little baby
and I will love you to the end of my days.
~ Excerpt from Carlotta Sullivan's memory journal

The rain continued long into the night and the next day. It let up slightly in the afternoon and they decided to make a break for town.

Jed took the horses out and hooked the doctor's horse to his buggy. Dr. Casey let Jed and Lillian go on ahead. Lillian tried to push her horse faster, but Jed warned her against it.

"With all that rain, the road is going to be muddy and there might be some mudslides. We want to move a bit slower than normal."

Lillian nodded but didn't say anything.

"You've been awfully quiet."

"Sorry."

"Are you okay?"

She sighed. "Yes. I was really hoping Dr. Casey would at least listen to us about the Bible, but he didn't seem to really care about any of it."

"You've shared the gospel with lots of people over the last few weeks and had good responses. I think only having one or two in that amount is a good thing. You can't get discouraged over one person saying no."

"Except he didn't even say no. He didn't say anything. I want to be alone with my thoughts."

Jed didn't respond and Lillian glanced at him. He was looking at her, concern written all over his face. He finally nodded and kept his mouth shut the rest of the way home.

Once at the Stuart home, Lillian helped brush the horse down and then went straight to her room. She didn't want to ever come out but knew she would have to for supper. She tried to read her Bible, but even her favorite verses weren't helping. She tried to pray, but every word she said fell flat. Instead, she pulled out her mother's journal and started reading it from the beginning again. She read through half of it before Abigail came to get her for supper.

Lillian went through the motions of being happy and having good conversations with the family, but her heart wasn't in it at all. The rain had continued through the meal and that night. When she got up in the morning, the first thing she heard was the rain pounding on the roof overhead. There would be no book route today. Perhaps Ivory needed help at the library. It would be worth a dash over there if she could borrow an oilskin to stay somewhat dry.

She borrowed Pastor Stuart's oilskin and ran through the muddy street to the Building. Once in the door, she quickly took the large garment off and hung it up on the coat rack. The Building seemed deathly quiet. Was no one here? She knew Lena for sure had to be, but where was Ivory? She should hear the chattering of Miss Bledsoe already. Even if Ivory was alone, she seemed to talk to herself just to make conversation.

Or something. She was so different from Lena. Where Ivory was open and talkative, Lena was private and silent as a mouse, maybe quieter actually. Then there was Edna. Edna was harder to figure out. She was so different from anyone else Lillian had ever seen.

Lillian made her way to the library and found it dark. No one had lit any lamps or candles. She searched around the large room in every nook and cranny. She finally found someone sitting near a window reading a book. "Lena?" she called out tentatively. She was fairly certain Lena was the only person who would be reading in the library at this early hour, but wasn't sure.

The person looked up. "Yes? Oh, Lillian, what are you doing here?"

"I had to get out of the house and couldn't go on my route." Lillian moved closer and stood looking out the large window. "Have you ever seen so much rain before?"

Lena closed her book. "No, not this bad. We get a lot of rain here, but not usually for this long."

Lillian sighed. "Is there anything that needs to be done here at the library?"

Lena chewed her lower lip. "Not unless I missed something yesterday. I went through every shelf to make sure the books were all in the right places. They were. I also put the books that had come in recently back on the shelves. And dusted."

Lillian looked around. "This is such a pretty room."

"Mm-hm."

"Any ideas on what I can do to be productive?"

"Read?"

Lillian choked on a laugh. "How is that productive?"

Lena shrugged with a smile. "It might not be as productive as cooking a meal for someone, but it is expanding your mind."

"I suppose. Any suggestions?"

"Have you read *Pride and Prejudice*?"

"Only about five times."

Lena gave a shy giggle. "Have you checked out any of the books Ivory brought with her?"

"A few, but not many. Why?"

"There's a few I hadn't heard of before. Come. I'll show them to you."

"I heard voices," someone interrupted them. "I thought maybe it was the Moon Witch."

Lillian turned to see Mrs. Branson, the owner. "Do you mean Ivory?"

"Yes."

"Is she not here?" Lena asked.

"I ain't seen her since she was here with Curt t'other day. I told that Curt to keep her in this library and out of my kitchen. Can't have her putting spells on the food or nothing. But I ain't seen her since and don't care to." She huffed and turned away.

As soon as her footsteps faded, Lillian faced Lena again. "I had heard talk of a Moon Witch but didn't realize everyone was talking about Ivory."

"Mr. Armstrong told me folks around here don't like her much."

Lillian averted her eyes. No wonder Ivory had requested to talk to her at that meeting. Why hadn't she put more stock in that request and reached out to Ivory since then? She shouldn't focus only on those who weren't Christians. Sometimes Christians needed a good friend, too.

Lillian and Lena spent the rest of the day talking a little and reading more. They had a small lunch Mrs. Branson reluctantly provided, and Lillian tried to converse with the prickly owner, but she would have none of it. By the time an hour before supper rolled around, the rain still hadn't let up and they hadn't seen a single soul besides themselves.

"I need to go back. If it is still raining tomorrow, maybe we can do this again."

"Maybe," Lena said.

"Do you want to come with me? The oilskin should be big enough for both of us. I'm sure the Stuarts wouldn't mind you coming for supper, and you could share my bedroom tonight."

Lena smiled shyly. "Thank you for the offer, but I would rather stay here."

"Okay. Don't take this wrong, but I hope I don't see you tomorrow."

"I agree. I would rather be out on my routes than stuck in this big building. Even though I love to read."

"Goodnight, Lena."

"Goodnight, Lillian."

The rain finally stopped a couple days later, and Lillian gladly went out on her routes and back to her normal routine. With one minor change. Well, some would consider it major, but to her right now it was only minor. She didn't talk about God unless someone else brought Him up. She couldn't. No matter how big the openings were, she froze and moved on before she could say anything about God.

Opal had asked her if she had shared anything recently, and Lillian couldn't even give her an answer. She said something vague about sharing with the doctor a week or so ago.

"Have you had so few opportunities?"

Lillian shrugged.

"What is going on?"

"What do you mean?"

Opal put her hands on her hips. "Ever since the storm, you haven't been yourself. What happened?"

"Nothing."

"Something happened or you wouldn't be acting this way."

"I'm fine. I shared the gospel with someone and they completely rejected it. That's all."

"And that is what has you so down?"

"I don't know. I guess so."

"Lillian, that's going to happen. You told me a while back that not everyone will accept Christ. It isn't a failure on your part; it is their failure."

"I know, but I still feel like it is my fault."

Opal looked at her but didn't say anything more. Lillian didn't need her to. She knew what Opal was thinking. This pride in believing she had anything to do with the doctor's rejection was worse than her pride in thinking she couldn't share the gospel because of how shy she was.

"I need to go finish my route."

"I will be praying for you."

Lillian smiled her response and hurried on her way.

18

My dearest Lillian, I don't have long left for this life. I am currently holding you on my chest while I dictate this to Malachi. I want you to know that you did not cause me to die. You gave me hope. Life. A purpose for the past few months. Many women die in childbirth. It is a dangerous but wonderful thing to give birth to a living human being. As I stare at your cute button nose and wispy dark hair, I am filled with awe at how God designed things.

My dearest Lillian, you are loved. Never forget that fact. Goodbye, my little darling daughter. Take care of your father for me. I love you both so much. But, Lord willing, I will see you both again someday in heaven.

~ Excerpt from Carlotta Sullivan's memory journal

$\mathcal{L}$illian, we need to talk," Patience said. It was almost two weeks since the rains. The bridge linking their town to the outside world had washed away in the subsequent flooding, and it was too soon to begin rebuilding it.

"About what?"

"You."

"I can't get out of town, so you can't be asking me to leave."

"No. We love having you here, but we are also getting concerned. You had such a lovely smile when you came here, and your joyful attitude is something everyone noticed. But ever since the rains you haven't been the same. You have been sullen, moody, and even quieter than before. What happened in Mrs. McFeely's cabin?"

"Nothing happened."

"That isn't completely true," Patience stated. "Jed told us everything that happened there and that includes how your mood changed shortly after you arrived. Is there something between you and the doctor that would cause this sudden change?"

"Something between us? What are you implying?"

"Do you like him?"

Lillian flinched as her eyes widened. "No. Absolutely not."

"Ah. So you greatly dislike him. And that is why you didn't want to be stuck in the cabin with him."

"Yes. That and the dead body."

"Anything else?"

Lillian shrugged.

"That isn't a real answer," Patience said. "You are a grown woman, so I won't go lecturing you like I would with my children. Just know that I am here for you if you ever want to talk. I know you have something bothering you and I hoped you would open up to me about it. Apparently I was wrong."

"I'm a failure," Lillian blurted out as Patience began to stand.

Patience sat back down hard. "A failure at what?"

"Everything."

She looked at Lillian with disbelief in her eyes. "I don't think that is true. Be more specific."

"I am a failure as a Christian, a librarian, a friend, a daughter. I wanted to make my mother proud, but I think all I have done is disappoint her more than I possibly could have if I had tried to."

"How do you figure that? You have grown up into a lovely young woman who cares deeply about people."

"Not anymore."

"What do you mean not anymore?"

"Just that. I don't care about people anymore. I used to feel something for the people I went to meet, but now I don't. I just want to finish delivering the books and be done with my day."

"Why do you think that changed?"

"I don't know."

"I think you do."

Lillian shook her head.

"I think it has something to do with being stuck in a cabin with Jed and the doctor for almost a full day. I get that. Being stuck alone in a cabin full of men would probably do something to me, too. Men should be out doing things, not cooped up in a tiny house with nothing to do. At least you had some cleaning you could do. They had nothing."

"Besides their checkers."

Patience smiled. "Jed does love a good game of checkers. But that wasn't all, was it?"

Lillian ground her teeth. "No."

"Then what else was there?"

"Why are you so good at this?"

"I am a mother and the wife of a pastor. I need to be good at asking the right questions."

Lillian sighed. "I failed at sharing the gospel with the doctor."

"Why is that your failure?"

"Because I did it for the wrong reasons."

"What was your reason?"

"To make him nicer."

Patience fought a smile and lost. "You've read the whole Bible at least once, right?"

"Yes."

"Then you should know that there are many godly men and women who failed many times over. And God still used them. Some of them even did things for the wrong reason and had God work things around for good."

Lillian scowled. "I know all of that. What does that have to do with me?"

"Because you are being too stubborn to see that God can use you for this despite what you call a failure. Just because the doctor was too hardhearted to see that you were sharing something amazing with him does not mean you were a failure. And your reasons aside, any time you share the gospel with someone, you risk being rejected. You have to learn to not take it personally."

"And not take it out on others."

Patience nodded.

"Thank you. I'll think about that."

"And pray?"

Lillian sighed. "And pray."

"Good."

Lillian retreated to her bedroom, where she opened up her Bible and started reading parts of the Old Testament and then moved to the New Testament. She finally set it aside as it grew too dark to see from the light of the window.

She knelt by her bed and folded her hands. "God, I haven't been living the way I should. Everything was going so well for a while. Did I let pride creep in again and ruin things for me?" She paused. "Probably. I need Your help, God. I can't do this on my own. I want to get back to the way I was before. Tell me what to do."

As she said the words, a verse popped into her mind.

Trust in the Lord with all thine heart and lean not unto thy own understanding. In all your ways acknowledge Him and He shall direct thy paths.

"I trust You, God. Help me to trust You more and more every day. I want what You want for me. No matter what others think or say about what I do and say. I want to be Your servant again on the trail. I want to smile again the way everybody remembers me from when I came here. I want to live life the way I did before all this death and destruction. I trust You to do what is needed."

Peace filled her as she prayed and she let out a contented sigh. "Thank You, God."

The End

Historical Note

Librarians on muleback or horseback? Did it really happen?

In the 1930s, the United States had drooped into the Great Depression, a severe economic downturn. As part of his response, President Franklin Roosevelt instituted the Works Progress Administration (WPA), which sought to provide employment and opportunity for Americans, especially those in poverty-stricken areas. A WPA project, the Pack Horse Library Program began in 1936 with the goal of employing women and spreading literacy in the rural Kentucky Appalachians, an area that the Depression had hit hard.

Each county had several librarians – usually local women (and a few men), who worked out of a small library. Local school boards normally supported the library by providing rent, heat, and electricity (if available), with the understanding that the library would aid the school with resources. One main librarian usually stayed at the library building itself; he or she was often responsible for sorting and repairing the materials. The other librarians headed out on the trail, packing books and magazines into their saddlebags.

Every packhorse librarian (sometimes called a "bookwoman") received a section of the county for which she was held responsible. This section was divided into a set of routes. The WPA required the librarians to ride their routes twice a month – thus, a bi-weekly rotation – with each librarian riding over one hundred miles a week – uphill and downhill, through swollen creeks and dangerous weather. The librarians provided their own horse or mule and received a monthly salary of $28 – an adequate wage at the time.

The Pack Horse Program attracted attention from schools, churches, and social groups outside the Appalachian area. These groups donated money and materials to the program, which tremendously grew within a year as mountain folk became accustomed to having literature available that opened their eyes to a world outside the Appalachians. In 1943, with the United States' entrance into WWII, the Pack Horse Library Program officially closed, but the legacy of literature which the bookwomen brought to the mountains lived on.

Amanda Tero

A Strand of Hope

Lena Davis is the daughter her mom never wanted.

But she survived. Through stories. Because books didn't judge. Books weren't angry she was alive. Books never expected her to be anything but who she was.

As she grows up, her beloved library becomes her true home.

So when the library is designated part of President Roosevelt's Packhorse Library Project, Lena is determined to get the job of bringing books to highlanders, believing she'll finally be free of her mom forever.

But earning the trust of highlanders is harder than she imagined, and her passion for books might not be enough to free her from her chains.

amandatero.com

A.M. Heath

Hearts on Lonely Mountain

Can two lonely people find more than a fleeting friendship or will a prejudiced town keep them apart?

When Ivory Bledsoe left the city to minister to the people of the rural mountain town of Willow Hollow, she never expected to be shunned rather than welcomed. Seeing the town as a lost cause, she's eager to return home, but when the bridge leading out of own is washed away during a flood, she finds herself stranded in the last place she wants to be.

Ben Thrasher was content with his quiet life until he met the new librarian. He can't help but be drawn to the friendly and lively Ivory Bledsoe, despite her being at the center of the town's latest superstition. It's only a matter of time until she captures his heart, turning his world upside down in the process.

Has Ivory gotten God's plan for her all wrong or is there still a way she can serve these people? And can Ben ask her to stay in a place where so few are willing to embrace her?

christianauthoramheath.net

Alicia G. Ruggieri

The Secret Place of Thunder

The mountains have imprisoned her long enough...

Edna Sue O'Connell came back to the Kentucky hills out of duty and can't wait for the chance to escape again. Her work as a horseback librarian in rural Appalachia provides enough income for her invalid father to survive in the midst of the Great Depression, but it affords her with little else.

When an opportunity arises for Edna to take on an additional book delivery area, she spies a glimmer of hope that she might find a way out of Willow Hollow after all... and that she might actually make something of her life apart from the tragedy that has filled it thus far.

But the new routes give Edna more than she ever bargained for. Slowly, she finds that the mountains contain many valuable secrets – if she has the grit to meet them.

aliciagruggieri.com

About the Author

Faith Blum is a small-town Wisconsin girl. She has independently published over 25 books in over five years. Most of her books are Christian Historical Fiction with an emphasis on Westerns. During an eBook sale, she was #2 overall in Kindle eBooks on Amazon.

Faith resides in Central Wisconsin with her husband, son, and their cat, Smokey. When not writing, you can find her cooking, doing dishes, sewing, reading, or spending time with her husband and son. She loves to hear from her readers, so feel free to contact her on her website: https://faithblum.com.

Made in the USA
Middletown, DE
22 July 2024

57867459R00080